BRIDE OF THE NILE

ROSALYN KENDRICK wrote her first novel at 24 when her son was a baby. Her first published book, *Does God Have a Body? and Other Questions*, appeared in 1977. With her earnings from the book she started her travels by going to Jerusalem. She has since travelled extensively throughout the Middle East, including Egypt, Jordan, Morocco, Turkey and Petra. She converted to Islam and has written several books on the subject, including recommended GCSE texts. On a trip to Pakistan in August 1989, she met the man who is now her husband, although when they first met neither spoke the other's language. To date she has had thirty books published, with seven others in the pipeline, including a travel guide to Petra. *Bride of the Nile* is her first published fiction.

To my mother

Bride of the Nile

Rosalyn Kendrick

WOLFHOUND PRESS

First published in 1998 by
Wolfhound Press Ltd
68 Mountjoy Square
Dublin 1, Ireland
Tel: (353-1) 874 0354
Fax: (353-1) 872 0207

© 1998 Rosalyn A. Kendrick

This book is fiction. All characters, incidents and names have no connection with any persons living or dead. Any apparent resemblance is purely coincidental.

Wolfhound Press receives financial assistance from the Arts Council/ An Chomhairle Ealaíon, Dublin, Ireland.

British Library Cataloguing in Publication Data
A catalogue record for this book is available from the British Library.

ISBN 0-86327-622-9

Cover Painting: Eva Byrne
Cover Design: Estresso
Typesetting: Wolfhound Press
Printed and bound by the Guernsey Press Co. Ltd., Guernsey, Channel Islands.

Chapter One

Rosanna March gazed in frank disbelief at the tall, glowering youth who was propping up the desk in the arrival bay. He was making precious little effort to be welcoming, despite the fact that he had just called her name and mouthed the magic words 'Welcome to Egypt'.

She flung down her case in sheer exasperation. It wasn't that there was anything sinister or objectionable in the fierce face that impatiently looked her over. In fact, he was a very handsome young man and Rosanna eyed him up and down with more than a flicker of interest. But if that was supposed to be a welcome, it was about as warm as a packet of frozen peas, and she did not trust him.

He was lean and graceful, and Rosanna estimated his age at about twenty, a few years older than herself — she was sixteen. His shirt, open at the neck, revealed skin tanned as dark as the Egyptians' around him. Anyone might have assumed he was an Egyptian himself were it not for one startling feature — his eyes were a sharp, piercing blue. Apart from that, he had the same languid look and the same beautifully-shaped mouth, but she got the distinct impression that he practised sneering at people.

Rosanna knew that her forehead and upper lip were soaked with sweat, that her shirt was sticking uncomfortably to her body, that there was a large dirty streak on the right leg of the white cotton trousers she had foolishly decided to wear for travel. At that moment she could not

5

have described herself as anything other than crumpled, whereas she should have been bright and perky, and bursting with enthusiasm for the adventure she had earned as the result of such hard work — a free place on a tour of major Egyptian sites, with lectures by Professor Edison of Barnard University, whose recent excavations and theories on the Osiris cult had caused much controversy.

The problem was, this youth did not look anything like the expert on Egyptian antiquity Rosanna had been expecting. An Egyptologist should be something between a bank manager in a dark suit and Indiana Jones. This unpleasant pin-up boy was far too young, wore faded denims and an equally faded jacket over a plain black T-shirt, and had the unmistakable lilt of an Irish accent.

'You're not Harry Edison!' she accused him, trying to stop her voice coming out like a wail. He shifted his weight to his other hip, but did not take his elbow off the desk. He looked slightly weary, slightly bored. He ran his eyes down the list of names on the clipboard in front of him.

'However, may I assume that you *are* Miss March?' he said, without looking at her. 'Of Brandon High?'

'Yes.' Rosanna swallowed nervously. She knew her essay on the Eighteenth Dynasty, which had made her a prize-winner for the whole southern half of England, had earned her a sort of mini-VIP status; but she was not used to people calling her 'Miss March'. It seemed flattering, somehow, and she grinned. 'Yes, that's me.'

'Well, I'm glad you've arrived at the right place at last. We're all getting tired!' He picked up the clipboard and twanged the elastic. 'Shall we go? I'll explain on the way.'

Rosanna looked round, but there was no sign of any other young Egyptologist prizewinners.

'Excuse me!' She placed her feet firmly apart and refused to budge. 'I certainly am tired, but I didn't come all the way to Cairo to be hijacked by some Irishman! How do I know you're not one of those characters that hang around airports, trying to lure girls away to sell as slaves? I'm not going anywhere with you until you identify yourself and tell me what has happened to Harry Edison.'

The hijacker had not actually made any noticeable attempt to make her go anywhere. He was already on his way to the exit, leaving her to manage her own suitcase. He stopped. Rosanna did not actually hear his impatient sigh, but she felt it. He turned and considered her mutinous face for a moment.

'Please?' She smiled at him, politely. There was a long pause before he smiled back.

'I'm sorry, Miss March. I'm the one who's over-tired. I was up all last night — but that's none of your concern, of course. I'm afraid I've got a disappointment for you. You're not going to be a white slave, and you're not going to get Harry Edison after all. He's ill, and I've been drafted in instead. The name's O'Neill. Finbar O'Neill.'

'Ill?' Rosanna was aghast. 'What do you mean, ill?'

'The same thing that everyone else means — only in his case, of course, being such a celebrity, he's probably enjoying the attentions of a dozen pretty nurses and alternating his nasty medicine with champagne.'

'I don't believe this!' She was so disappointed she could feel her throat tightening. 'What's the matter with him? Why weren't we told?'

Finbar O'Neill's lips quirked downwards a fraction. He didn't look the least bit apologetic — more amused.

'Crazy as it must sound to you, Miss March, I'm afraid there wasn't time. Edison was virtually on his way here to meet all his adoring sycophants this afternoon, when he decided to treat himself to a last swim. He's been living it up at the new seaside resort in Hurghada on the Red Sea. I expect you've heard of it?' Rosanna shook her head, dumbly. 'The joke is that one of the poisonous fish there hadn't been told about our Harry's fame and importance. It stung him, same as it would any other fool who went out beyond

7

the markers. His leg's gone a funny colour and swollen up, and he has to rest and recuperate until it all subsides.'

'Well, surely — if it's not serious — won't he be able to join us later?' Hope rose briefly, only to be flattened by the youth's malevolent grin. He actually seemed to derive satisfaction from the situation.

'Afraid not. He's pulled out. Cairo University, in its infinite wisdom, has seen fit to reward all my sterling past work for them by offering me this wonderful opportunity to take his place. I've been put in charge of this tour. Sorry, and all that, but you'll just have to make do with me.'

'This can't really be happening!' Rosanna muttered. 'Somebody up there must have it in for me.'

She realised she was being unfair, overreacting, as usual. It was hardly this stranger's fault.

'Well, there it is,' he said, evenly. 'What do you want me to do? Get you a seat on the next plane back?'

'Don't be ridiculous.'

'Miss March — I'm too tired, and too busy, to stand here arguing with a stubborn little schoolgirl all night. Are you coming or aren't you?'

'What did you say your name was?' Her voice was ice-cold.

'Finbar O'Neill, madam. O-N-E-I-L-L.' He spelled it out with deliberate contempt. 'Aren't you going to make a note of it?'

Rosanna knew her hands were shaking, partly with shock and partly from sheer exhaustion. She hoped he would not see. 'Mr O'Neill,' she began, keeping tight control, 'I may be a schoolgirl, but that doesn't give you the right to be offensive to me. I can't see any other people who look like expedition members, and in any case, I'm sure I can't be the only one to be disappointed about Harry Edison. You must know that meeting such a famous expert was one of the main elements of our prize!'

'I can assure you, Miss March, that if I had been capable

of persuading Edison to get up off his backside ... Unfortunately the great man is ill, and that's it. You're lucky to have me.'

'Lucky? I was wondering if we were — were entitled to some sort of refund.'

She regretted the words instantly. O'Neill's eyes widened in genuine disbelief, then narrowed to slits. The jaw came up, the lines hardened.

'Miss March, I have a party of kids waiting to be booked into the hotel. I'm nearly out on my feet. Come along, now, be a good girl and don't give me any more trouble. I've got work to do. Understand?'

'But —'

'It's either that or you can sleep here at the airport. Now, don't be a silly girl. Come along and get your beauty sleep, then tomorrow you can flash your claws at me all you want.'

Rosanna noticed that faces were beginning to blur, the floor beginning to slide away. She swallowed.

'I —'

The next few moments were a hazy jumble of sensations. Colours flashed, nausea came and went, her legs disappeared, her body dissolved. Her nose was pressed into the roughness of a denim jacket. She opened her eyes. A silver button gleamed just beyond her nose. She became aware that she did have legs, and was in fact standing on them. Just. She put up a hand and pushed.

'Let go of me,' she whispered. 'I'll be all right now.'

'There's gratitude for you.'

She looked up at O'Neill's face. He was grinning. 'You can fall into my arms any time you like, baby. Any time you like.'

'I'm sorry,' Rosanna mumbled, too tired even to be embarrassed. 'I've had enough, that's all.'

'Of course you have,' he smiled. 'Come along now, Miss March, and do what Finbar tells you. Everything'll be OK.

9

You'll see. Can you walk?'

'I — I think so. Yes, of course I can.' She straightened up. O'Neill picked up her case.

'OK?' he asked. Rosanna nodded. Satisfied that she could make it, he turned once more for the exit. 'Follow me.'

* * *

Lying in the much-advertised comfort of the Cairo hotel bedroom, Rosanna fought off her exasperation and stretched out sensuously, enjoying the fine cotton sheets, the sheer luxury of the white silk bedspread, the gilt cherubs holding up glass lamps. Three little flies made patterns noiselessly, endless movements into triangles, as if they were bound together by invisible elastic.

This was Egypt — and she was really here. In a bed like this, she wouldn't have minded being a queen of Egypt, one of those glittering hostesses to emperors, powerful manipulators of their brother-husbands, wealthy beyond imagination; spoilt darlings for whom countless soldiers gave their lives and countless peasants toiled to make monuments.

Rosanna abandoned herself to visions of brown gleaming bodies straining in the sun, heaving the huge blocks up to a half-made pyramid, under a searing blue sky.

Chapter Two

I wish he would not keep me waiting like this. He does it deliberately. He knows I have been waiting for what seems like hours, in this heat, just to snatch a few moments with him.

It is the time of the rising, and the sun overhead strikes like a hammer. I have come to the brink of our Nilometer; down the vast circular shaft, the green water sucks and gurgles far below. The Nilometer was sunk at the end of this shaded walkway beyond the palace gardens by my father, the god. It is one of the biggest in all the two kingdoms. He did that deliberately, of course. Anything less would have been inconceivable. I watched them build it, the huge pit sinking down into the rich black soil, the living land bestowed and owned by him.

They say that at the sources of the Nile, away in the high plateaux of the Land of Ghosts, torrents of tropical rain are descending, smiting the trees of the forests and pouring forth the life-giving waters which will drown and then fertilise our fields. Peasants are already leaving their land and their homes, moving to the safety of the hills. They won't starve. Most of them will find employment in my father's building projects, while the floods cover and replenish their fields.

At least this god-king makes some effort for his people, unlike his predecessors — but it is his philosophy that if he is to provide them with bread, beer and onions, then they shall work for it. And work they do, toiling with the massive blocks until they fall from exhaustion and have to be pulled from under the feet of the heaving men, and dumped in the meagre shade. Many die. It seems to be inevitable. No one asks many questions. The land needs the flood, after all. It is not a free gift of the gods. There is always a price.

Now, out of the corner of my eye, I can see him; at the end of the walkway he pulls his chariot to a halt with his usual military smartness. His two horses are black and shining with sweat. He doesn't like to stand still, my lovely prince, the commander of the Ra-Sutekh division; and neither do his horses. Look at them complaining, their feathered head-dresses dipping up and down as they snort. He snaps his fingers to make the servant come running, take nervous hold of the beasts and lead them to the water-trough.

He leaps down, pulls off his gauntlets of white leather and tosses them nonchalantly into the chariot. He is looking round; perhaps he is wondering where I am.

I step forward, and he sees me — I can feel this, although he gives no sign. His short cloak, woven with gold threads amongst the purple, flashes in the sun. He pushes it back over his shoulder, letting the god's rays strike the Golden Fly, the Grand Order of Merit, which gleams on his shoulder.

He is staring down the length of the walkway, towards me, hands on hips — but now a priest comes shuffling from the Temple of Thoth to talk to him. Their heads bob together, the old man's shaven and round like a gleaming egg, my prince's jutting and proud, with the black Horus lock, worn by all princes born of the blood of the god, curling at the side.

I know he is always courteous to the priests, but I have waited long enough. I walk away from the Nilometer, down to the thick rushes that fringe the edge of the river. He will know where to find me. It is a nuisance that there are priests here, too, up to their knees in the muddy ooze, examining the baskets that have been wedged on the bank during the night, by silent women, or have grounded there as the current took them.

They don't land there by chance. There's a bend in the river and an outcrop of black rock that causes the current to swirl this way. Any baskets that haven't sunk, or smashed on the jutting rocks, or been swept out to the Great Sea, drift into this bay and come to rest in the rushes and Nile lilies and black mud beneath the priests' quarters.

And the priests come here, at their leisure, to look for boys, or very occasionally — when they have need or have been paid something on the sly — for girls. No questions asked. None needed. Just a fumbling amongst the pathetic containers to discover which have remained waterproof, which have landed right side up, which, if any, contains a useful boy to join the other nameless, fatherless children who are all given the name 'Moses', or 'drawn out' of the river.

The priests look glum. I expect they were hoping for a boy-child this morning, but there aren't any. All the babies are dead, except one, whose pathetic cries barely have the strength to reach my ears. I don't like to watch: the senior priest just pushes the basket under with his foot. I hope the poor mother is not there, somewhere in the reed beds, watching.

I have often wondered what desperation drives these mothers to take their infants, daughters usually, and cast them upon the Nile like this. They say it is kinder to do this, to place the child's fate in the hand of the god, rather than simply to expose it, or bury it in the sand, because of their poverty.

His soft voice whispers suddenly behind me, making me jump.

'Generations will be born and die, nations will rise and fall, but we are eternal.'

His uncanny ability to read my thoughts, his warm hands touching my shoulders, make me shiver with delight. I sink down with him amongst the rushes. I don't care if the priests see us. Let them see! My soul is consumed with desire for this golden youth who is touching me, stroking my arms. It doesn't matter if he sees my desire for him. He knows everything about me, knows that I would willingly die for him if he required it. I kiss his cheek, turning his face towards me, seeking his mouth.

'We are only dust.' I have to say it. His words had a careless confidence that a god might not overlook.

13

His fierce kiss takes away my speech. His hands grip me, his fingers dig into me, as if our youth and our love might suddenly be snatched away.

Will it always have to be like this, stealing feverish moments secretly in the reed beds at the midday hour while the world is sleeping? Look, I am crying — not from pain, not from any sadness, but from sheer joy that you should want me, that you have chosen me from all the girls and princesses who cast eager eyes upon your beauty.

He laughs. 'We are not dust,' he whispers. 'We are eternal. Would you leave me now?' He takes my chin in his hand, forcing me to look at him. 'Would you?'

'No. Never! Not in this lifetime.'

He laughs again. 'Our lifetimes are billions of years.'

I make a fist and punch him lightly. He is far too proud, this son of the god. It makes me nervous. Quickly I repeat the old formula to avert evil.

'We are dust.'

* * *

One moment they were together, hidden in the reeds; the next he was gone. Like a ghost. Her arms, clutched across her bosom, could still feel him, but they were empty. How could he have slipped away while they had been holding each other so close? She could not believe he was no longer there.

Rosanna reached out automatically and switched on the lamp. For a moment panic coursed through her veins as she gaped round at the unfamiliar surroundings, not knowing where she was. She sat up, perplexed. She was in a bed, and her eyes focused on a gilt cherub holding up a glass lampshade.

Then she remembered. She had heard of people pinching themselves to see if they were really awake, and had considered it a rather silly thing to do. Now, she pinched herself.

She looked at her watch. Only 6.15. Breakfast had been scheduled for ten o'clock, to give the late arrivals a chance to recover from their journeys. That gave Rosanna several hours to kill. She supposed that those who were not bursting with excitement at the thought of being in Egypt were sensibly snoozing away. She could no more sleep than fly.

Bold plans began to nudge their way into her head. There was nothing in the world she would enjoy more than going to the banks of the Nile and watching the sun come up in the company of that ancient river and her own thoughts and dreams.

She picked up her shoulder bag and stuffed her purse and papers into it, opened the door, and marched resolutely up the corridor.

Chapter Three

Dawn was pearling the horizon with soft grey light as Rosanna bent over the lapping wavelets of the Nile, her eyes creased with concentration. Finding a quiet corner somewhere so that she could get out her notebook and record a few first impressions had not been easy, for being alone and being in Cairo simply did not go together.

Crossing the city had been a nightmare. Even at that hour, the bus shelter was seething like an overturned hive, and Rosanna could see no taxis, but someone with a smattering of English pointed her towards a battered old Chevrolet up a rubbish-strewn side-street. She picked her way through the debris to where it waited, with an air of defiance, amongst the miscellany of vehicles, people and donkeys that clogged the road. She supposed she was in luck.

On the corniche along the riverside things were quieter. The Nile, on its inexorable way to the delta and out to the great sea beyond, was a thick dark green. Rosanna wandered along the corniche for about half a mile, enjoying the breeze in her face, the smell of the water.

She had been down to the bank of the Thames several times, but she had forgotten the smell of water, and the sounds a river makes, purling, trickling; forgotten the feeling of awe in standing quite still and watching as the mighty power of an old river surged by.

Joyfully she went down one of the many staircases to the water's edge, slipped off her sandals, and dabbled her toes in the Nile. She wanted to embrace the river, to sing. It was ridiculous, but she felt the tears on her cheeks.

'Well, well, well! What do we have here? Little Miss March, if I'm not mistaken.'

Rosanna screwed up her eyes to focus on the unwelcome figure of Finbar O'Neill standing at the top of the steps, leaning against the corniche rail, a cigarette dangling nonchalantly from his lips. He looked as if he might have been there for hours.

'Good morning, Mr O'Neill,' she muttered. Of all the multitude of possible places she could have been, of all the teeming millions of people whose paths she might have crossed, it had to be him, and it had to be here. He tossed away the stub of his cigarette, vaulted over the rail and ambled down towards her.

'And what, might I ask, do you think you're doing?' He sounded like a schoolmaster who had caught a pupil trying to pinch the exam papers in advance.

'I am sight-seeing, Mr O'Neill. This is the Nile, and I am looking at it.'

'Mmm. Still high and mighty, I see. I don't know, Miss March, it seems to me you're intending to cause me a whole load of trouble. Trouble I can do without. I left you safely tucked up in bed at the Hibis, didn't I?'

'Yes, but —'

'I did not, therefore, expect to find you gadding about on your own on the banks of the Nile. I suppose it hasn't occurred to your spoilt little brain, if there is one in there, that I am responsible for your safety?'

'I'm quite safe, Mr O'Neill.'

'And for the smooth running of the tour,' he continued. 'At what time, I wonder, might we have expected the pleasure of your company for breakfast?'

'Ten o'clock. As you instructed. I had no intention of being late.'

'Oh, really? And I suppose you can tell me in detail your

plan for getting yourself back to the hotel?'

'Well, no — but —'

'Have you ordered a taxi?'

'No. I could have got the man who brought me to wait for me, but —'

'I see.' O'Neill rolled his eyes in despair. 'Perhaps you intended to walk?'

'It's not far. I'm used to walking. I see no reason why I couldn't have walked.'

'What time did you set out?'

'Oh, just before seven o'clock.'

'And it is now?'

Rosanna looked at her watch, miserably. It was just nine o'clock.

'I would have made it.' This interrogation was making her feel about six inches tall. O'Neill was tapping his foot against the step. He was not a patient man.

'I doubt it, Miss March. You have never been to Cairo before, I take it?'

'No. Never. I —' She was going to say it was the first time she had ever been abroad.

'Don't underestimate it,' he said curtly. 'This is not England, and you are nothing special — just another foreign tourist, another body in the crowd. You won't get preferential treatment here, on the streets, because you're English.'

A crimson flush crept up Rosanna's neck.

'How did you find me here?' she asked, changing the subject.

'Don't flatter yourself, my dear. To go looking for you was the very last thing that would have occurred to me. How was I supposed to know you had left the hotel?'

'I was wondering that.'

'I did *not* know. Now that I *do* know you have this thing about wandering off, I shall keep an eye on you in future.'

'Does it matter?'

'It may not matter to you, princess, but it does to me. If you get into difficulties, or actual danger, by being irresponsible, I shall not be too pleased about it. I'm paid to be in charge of you, whether you like it or not — to make sure that you and the other silly idiots don't actually hurt yourselves or get lost, raped or robbed.'

'I'm sorry, Mr O'Neill. I didn't think.'

O'Neill laughed. It was amazing the difference it made to his face.

Rosanna looked at him sideways. 'Well, what *are* you doing here, by the Nile?'

'Would you believe, the same as you?' He grinned, and reached for his cigarettes. He offered Rosanna one, but she shook her head. 'I came out here to see the dawn and enjoy a little bit of solitude. The fact that I've fallen over you is mere coincidence.'

'It must be a chance in a million.'

'Not really. Look!' He indicated the length of the riverbank. 'Lots of people come out early to take a stroll and clear their heads before the heat rises. It's amazing who you can bump into along the corniche. They say you can travel across half the world, and meet someone from the next street here.'

'I'm glad you found me, Mr O'Neill,' she said, shyly. 'I must admit, I did realise I'd bitten off a bit more than I could chew.'

'Well, that's promising. A glimmer of humility showing through. There's hope for you yet, Miss March.'

'I'll do my best.' Rosanna's smile was placating, but O'Neill had turned away from her and was gazing out towards Gezirah Island.

'It is beautiful, isn't it?' he murmured. 'It doesn't really matter how many times you come to the Nile, it's always like coming home.'

He turned, then, and looked at her. She could not tell whether his eyes, under the long lashes, were laughing in friendship or still contemptuous.

'Well — it just so happens that I do have a taxi coming for me,' he said. 'So you're lucky, aren't you?' Rosanna hung her head. 'Do you think you can manage to stay put and not do anything stupid while I pop up and see if it's arrived?'

Without waiting for her answer, he bounded up the steps and disappeared.

Rosanna gazed down at the flotsam that confused the river's edge, and then froze. Something had come into focus just below the surface of the water, something floating up amongst the detritus from the murky undertow.

She bent lower, trying to make out what it was, and suddenly realised with a shock of nausea that it was a human head. Even as she gasped in horror, the face slowly turned towards her — a dead, white, bloated face, the jaw hanging open. Rosanna jumped back with a cry.

Then a pebble hurtled past Rosanna's ear and the face became a thousand glittering fragments.

'Are you going to be all day?' came O'Neill's shout. 'What's the matter? Gone deaf all of a sudden?'

Rosanna looked again at the water, but there was nothing to be seen now, nothing but the litter of paper, wood, tinfoil, and empty cans.

Yet there had been a face, indistinct and shadowy, arching upwards through the water. She shivered despite the rising heat.

And there was something else. She could have sworn that, just as she jumped back, the swollen eyelids had opened and living eyes — dark, harsh, unblinking — had stared at her from that dead face.

Over her head, in the morning sky, sunrise lit up the huge bowl with pink and gold.

Chapter Four

Jean and Bertice Springer puffed heavily on their cigarettes and stared at Rosanna with disbelieving eyes.

'A face?'

'It was definitely a face,' Rosanna insisted, knowing that the whole thing sounded ridiculous. The girls smiled pityingly at her.

Professor Montagu Bloxham, Mike Cooper, and Joey Brown were the other occupants of their table. Bloxham was sipping thoughtfully at his lemon juice, and Mike was polishing the lenses of his expensive camera.

They had got through their introductions. Professor Bloxham was Australian, a senior lecturer and researcher at the Smithsonian in the USA; a stout man whose wrinkles were well on the way to becoming sags, he was obviously going to suffer quite a lot with the heat. Large sweatmarks were already spreading under his armpits and down the back of his cotton khaki jacket. They gathered he was big in mummification and ancient microbes. He had decided to join Harry Edison's tour for a holiday — 'busman's holiday,' as he put it. Jean Springer, like Rosanna, was a prize-winning amateur Egyptologist, and her parents had paid for her sister Bertice to go on the trip too. Jean was seventeen and Bertice fifteen. They both had short dark hair, neat Bermuda shorts in a fantasy of colours, and fashionable spectacles. They went in for scarlet lipstick and polished fingernails, and (behind their parents' backs) were heavy smokers.

Joey Brown was just a kid, all sandy hair and freckles, but obviously highly intelligent. He had won a prize in the junior section.

Mike Cooper was Australian, like the Professor, about sixteen, and — to judge from his traveller's tales and the amount of impedimenta he carried around — came from a very wealthy family. He had the self-assured air of a young man who had been to most places, and seen most of what he wanted to see. He was, in fact, 'fitting Egypt in' between a trip to Europe and an intended trip to Japan. He was by far the most attractive male in the party, and the upper half of his tanned and muscular body was displayed attractively, if none too subtly, in a bright yellow sweatshirt which read 'Shine on, Brisbane!'

'I guess you shouldn't have gone out on your own like that, Rosie,' he said, not looking up from his polishing.

'Not a very sensible thing to do at all, if you ask me,' muttered Jean, blowing a smoke ring. Jean did not strike Rosanna as being the last word in sympathy and patience. She had been the first to finish breakfast and had been fidgeting ever since. She had produced her compact and applied her red lipstick, twice.

'I didn't get where I am today by being sensible,' Rosanna sighed. 'I just thought —'

'You *didn't* think!' Jean drawled, aiming another smoke ring over the heads of the breakfast party and stubbing out her cigarette in an ashtray on the next table. Rosanna noticed how the stub, placed neatly against the others, bore the scarlet imprint of her lips. All in a row, like three little soldiers. 'You ought to have known better. Why didn't you ask one of us to go with you?'

'Come off it,' Bertice laughed. 'Rosie didn't know any of us to ask last night, did she? And in any case, I didn't notice you leaping around full of enthusiasm at dawn.'

'Heaven forbid! I meant at a more reasonable hour.'

'You can't move dawn to a more reasonable hour,' said Joey.

'You might have landed yourself in all sorts of difficulties,' observed the Professor, bravely taking pity on a small bread roll that had obviously lain neglected by previous customers for at least two days. He opened his little packet of apricot jam and spread it on thickly. It was his third bread roll. One had been all that Rosanna could force down. She was not in the mood for eating.

'Yes, indeed,' the Professor mused, relishing the last crumbs, 'all sorts of difficulties. Not least from your friend over there.'

He indicated O'Neill, breakfasting in splendid isolation at the far corner of the room. Rosanna knew that only too well. The thought increased her embarrassment. They all smoked, or chewed, meditatively.

'What do you make of him?' muttered Bertice. 'Not very friendly, is he? I hope he's going to brighten up when we get to know him.'

O'Neill must have heard her. He slowly turned his head and withered them with a contemptuous stare, before picking up his newspaper. It was the daily paper, in Arabic.

'You reckon you'll be all right, then, Rosie?' Joey was the only one who understood Rosanna's nerves and tiredness. She smiled at him gratefully.

'Yes, of course. It was just one of those passing things. I'm quite all right now.'

'You'd better be, if we're going to do the Museum,' said Jean sharply. Rosanna groaned. She could see what the girl was thinking. Jean didn't want her limelight occupied by invalids, fantasisers, hysterics, whatever. Rosanna left the table, irritated by the reaction of her new so-called friends. What had happened by the Nile had only been a moment's faintness and her over-tired brain throwing up something funny out of her imagination.

As if organised by some malevolent spirit, a white-

23

coated waiter chose that very moment to come bustling through the palms. Rosanna tried to step out of his way, and the edge of her bag caught O'Neill's glass of red carcadet tea and knocked it clean off the table. Controlling her impulse to swear, she bent down and picked it up, and fumbled in her bag for a tissue to mop up the spillage.

'Not your day, Miss March,' came the cool, arrogant voice. She looked up, blushing.

'I'm — I'm sorry,' she mumbled. 'It was an accident. I —'

'Leave it alone, for God's sake! The waiter will see to it.'

'Yes. I — of course.' Rosanna stood up. O'Neill was smiling, but it was a malicious smile. She wondered why on earth he had taken the job if he had no patience with flustered tourists.

'We'll be off in a few minutes,' he said. 'Do you think you might manage to get yourself ready on time? We really don't want to keep everybody waiting, do we?'

'Don't worry about me, O'Neill,' she muttered.

'I don't intend to,' he replied curtly, and buried his head in his paper.

* * *

'Hey! Mister Finbar, my friend!'

A tall, smiling man in a pale blue djellaba rushed forward to greet O'Neill as he stepped from their coach outside the Museum.

'Hassan! You old grave-robber!' They slapped hands and embraced. 'You're no friend of mine! Don't tell me you're still fooling them into keeping you employed.'

The man shook with laughter.

'Ah, Mister Finbar. Always you joke with Hassan. Hassan knows your little ways. When I heard you were coming ...'

He took O'Neill in his arms and squeezed him. Rosanna was amused. She would as soon have squeezed a cactus.

24

O'Neill was actually looking pleased, for once. 'Anything you need to know about Egypt,' he said, 'ask Hassan. He knows it all. He should do — he invented most of it himself.'

'Esteemed sir — what will these dear children think? Be patient with him, my honoured guests — he is a boy, and I am a hundred years old.'

It was nice to know that one person, at least, was not cowed by O'Neill's forbidding manner. Rosanna warmed to Hassan instantly.

'Hassan has fixed us up with a very good guide,' Finbar explained. 'A good practical guy called Mahmoud.'

Hassan's face clouded.

'Ah — Mister Finbar — Mahmoud — he is not to be.' He shuffled his feet with embarrassment.

'Come on, Hassan! You know I was relying on him.'

'Yes, I know it. But — it is sad —' Hassan shook his head. His leathery face was indeed so mournful that it looked as if he was about to cry. 'But don't worry. I have another guide for you. Do not fear. Everything is arranged.'

'Do I know the man? Can I work with him?'

'With whom can you not work, exalted one? Everyone loves you. Everyone is honoured to be of service to you.'

Rosanna spluttered into her handkerchief.

'The honour of being your guide has fallen to me.' A very smart Egyptian in a pin-striped suit and dazzling white shirt came across the foyer. Such hair as he had was oiled and neatly arranged across the balding dome of his head, and a smart, clipped moustache extended just to the edge of his lips and no further. Rosanna noticed that he had a gold tooth. 'My name is Abu Samil. I trust my services will be acceptable to you?'

O'Neill was not pleased. He was recoiling from Abu Samil with distaste.

'What's the matter with Mahmoud?' He spoke to Hassan, virtually cutting the newcomer dead.

'Did you not hear of it?' Abu Samil murmured, a flicker in his deep-set eyes. 'That delightful young man has fallen prey to the wicked Americans and their dollars. But what can you expect? To thrust a youth into the company of so much money, so much glitter ...' He sneered the words. 'The temptation was too much for him.'

'What do you mean?' O'Neill was running out of patience.

'I'm afraid your friend has been sent to serve a prison sentence, Mr O'Neill. He protested his innocence, of course, but some evidence was found against him that the police could not overlook. Most distressing.'

'Oh, wonderful!' muttered Jean Springer. 'Another last-minute replacement. A great tour this is going to be!'

Abu Samil looked at her coldly.

'Such is the will of the gods,' he said.

Rosanna could not resist it. 'Surely you mean the will of Allah?'

Abu Samil swung round and glared at her. For a moment his face showed nothing but pure venom; then, as if a cloth had been wiped over a blackboard, his annoyance disappeared and he was all charm again.

'As you say, my dear young lady.' He bowed to her, with a look of polite subservience.

They followed him into the massive marble halls.

Huge figures of granite, quartz and limestone ignored their eager stares and gazed over their heads, too lofty to acknowledge the existence of the insect-like humans crawling beneath them. These were the representations of men who knew that they were gods. Then there were the startlingly lifelike statues of the lesser mortals — the queens and royal women, the scribes, the household staff of kings.

Even O'Neill hurrying them on could not spoil Rosanna's delight. She began to feel quite proud of herself as she recognised one famous statue after another, and, under Abu Samil's approval, she began to feel that she really was a junior expert.

They paused before a gigantic statue of a powerful man clad only in a head-dress and loincloth. Rosanna knew him immediately.

'You see before you, my friends, His Majesty King Rameses II.' Abu Samil swept his arm in an expansive gesture, as if he were actually introducing them. 'Once the proudest of all the great monarchs of Egypt; now, alas, only a parcel of bones and dried flesh in the collection of royal mummies upstairs.'

'You mean, we can go up and see his actual corpse?'

Joey's macabre delight was shortlived.

'No, my dear sir. The corpse is indeed there, but not on show for you. That collection is now closed.'

'Hell, that's a shame!' Mike was disappointed too. 'I wouldn't have minded having a peek at the old guy. Eh, Rosie?'

Confronted with this Pharaoh's statue, however, Rosanna felt only distaste. She stared up at Rameses' fleshy, lascivious lips, curved in a slight sneer. Just looking at those stone lips, powerless now, made her shudder.

'Don't expect me to feel sorry for him!' she snapped sharply. 'He was a cruel old man.'

Her vehemence surprised them all. She had spoken with as much assurance as if she had known him personally.

'How do you know that?' teased Mike with a grin. 'I don't suppose he was worse than anyone else at that time.'

'Don't be fooled by this statue,' Rosanna said quietly. 'Look, they *always* show him as a virile young man, in his prime. They flatter him. He was an old man when they made this statue, but they didn't dare to show that. He would have killed them. He killed anyone who upset him.'

'You have made a special study of Pharaoh Rameses, perhaps, Miss March?' She turned to see Abu Samil examining her curiously, and blushed.

'No — I — I don't know where I got the information.'

'You must not believe all you read, madam. Many lies are told about our ancient history.'

'Most of them by your own countrymen,' laughed O'Neill. The guide bowed and nodded politely, but he did not look pleased. They all turned back to the statue.

'He had an exceptionally long reign, didn't he?' Rosanna commented. 'He never let go. I thought pharaohs were supposed to hand over the rule once their powers declined?'

'Sixty-seven years as king,' said Abu Samil, as proud of the achievement as if Rameses had been his own ancestor. 'He was a great pharaoh and a great warrior.'

'Just like a man to say so!' Jean scoffed. 'How much of that sixty-seven years was really *his* reign, I wonder?'

'He came to the throne as an infant,' said Rosanna.

'Then it would have been his mother who ruled until he came of age. Then I expect he married a powerful elder sister,' Jean interrupted. 'Most of those sixty-seven years he probably didn't have any real power at all.'

'Once again, you make a mockery of my simple statements, young ladies. You are right, of course. We guides are simple people. Our aim is not to stuff your pretty heads with indigestible facts and send you back to your hotels bored and exhausted. We wish only to please you, and perhaps give you a little to ponder and enjoy.'

The gang moved on, but Rosanna lingered. She wanted to make amends.

'Forgive us, Abu Samil. We didn't mean to be rude. You are an excellent guide.'

'It is kind of you to say so.'

'No, really, I mean it. Excellent. You've already opened our eyes to so many fascinating details.'

'And you have fascinated me, Miss March. You are so young to be one of the clever people who come here to teach us our business, and yet you have such a feeling for our past. I find the thought of English children being made to study *our* ancient history most intriguing. And gratifying.'

'Oh, we're not made to study it. Well, we might get a couple of lessons, usually about Tutankhamun, or a biblical bit about Moses leading the Israelites out of slavery. But there are plenty of books in the libraries for anyone who's interested. Like the Edison books,' Rosanna added, glowering at O'Neill. 'People only have to look. I did look. I felt somehow drawn to it.'

'Is that really so?' The guide's black eyes showed amusement. He had probably met hundreds of English girls who 'felt drawn to' Egypt.

'You can't stand here talking all morning,' O'Neill broke in. 'There's a lot more to see. Of course, there's nothing to stop you coming back here later, if you want to. A little trip on your own,' he added icily. Rosanna winced. 'But we do have the rest of the party to consider too, you know. They may have other ideas.'

'Of course. I'm sorry.' Rosanna coloured at the rebuke. She smiled ruefully at Abu Samil, and hurried off after the others.

* * *

By the time they entered the rooms set aside for the famous Tutankhamun exhibition, Rosanna found herself wishing they had come to this place first. They had seen so much already that these fresh splendours were almost too much to absorb. Mike apparently felt the same.

'I'm not doing all this justice,' he muttered. 'And dammit, this is the bit I really wanted to see!'

They had given up trying to listen to Abu Samil and were drifting from case to case by themselves. It was not the famous gold death-mask, nor the jewellery, which moved Rosanna most. She was enthralled by the display of Tutankhamun's baby vests and socks — all beautifully hand-stitched — and the dried remains of the floral wreaths which mourners had placed in his tomb. The tiny posy of wildflowers that someone had laid over his heart still bore traces of colour.

Mike was delighted to discover that Tutankhamun had had a fine collection of boomerangs that had been buried with him.

'Would you believe that?' he grinned. 'I thought only our Aussie Aborigines used them. D'you think they had kangaroos as well?'

'Maybe we should come back here later,' Rosanna suggested. 'In some of our free time. There's a limit to what you can take in on one occasion.'

Abu Samil was watching as they paused beside some intricately-carved alabaster vases that had been found stacked outside Tutankhamun's golden shrine.

'You like these?' he asked.

'I love it all. Every bit of it!' Rosanna told him.

'See, here!' He pushed a switch on the wall, and the vase in front of them was suddenly lit up from within. A previously invisible outline of the young king and his sister-queen appeared in the alabaster, shadowy figures still with a trace of colour. 'The ancients had skills we do not dream of.' He flicked the switch on and off a few times.

'Was this used as a lamp, then? It seems a bit nuts to shine a light through alabaster.'

'Perhaps, sir, the Pharaoh had no need of the bright lights you crave. But perhaps this lovely vase glowing in the dark comforted him in the loneliness of the small hours, or guided his footsteps back to his bed.'

'You mean, this was a night-light?' Rosanna giggled.

'Maybe he was afraid of the dark.'

'I prefer this one.' Rosanna pointed to a round bowl whose handles were a twining of graceful lotus blossoms and papyrus stems.

'Ah. Now there you have my favourite,' admitted Abu Samil. 'Do you see the band of lettering around the rim? It

30

was a message to the young king from someone who loved him dearly, and who could not bear his death.'

Rosanna's attention was riveted to it, and she became aware of a strange, cold feeling trickling down her spine. She bent down over the glass and examined the bowl closely.

'Excuse me,' she said quietly. 'Surely — surely this bowl doesn't belong with this collection?'

'What do you mean? All this was found in Tutankhamun's tomb.'

'But it wasn't made for him,' Rosanna persisted. 'This wasn't his bowl!'

Mike was laughing at her, but Abu Samil was smiling tolerantly. 'It surprises me,' he said, 'that a modern young lady should pick out this particular bowl to notice. It is very modest, compared to all the other things.'

It was. Just a simple bowl, a round of alabaster, with a message.

'Can you decipher this lettering?' She still could not tear her eyes away from it. Someone who loved him dearly. Someone who could not bear his death.

'I can, madam. Let me see.' Abu Samil paused for a moment and wrinkled his brow. Rosanna guessed he was summoning set phrases from memory, rather than reading the text. It was all part of the show.

'Live, O soul!' he began. 'Live for millions of years, O darling of Thebes.'

The bowl filled the case. It seemed to grow and swell even as Rosanna puckered her brow in concentration. It seemed, almost, to vibrate. A spasm of fear shook her. She grasped the strap of her shoulder-bag tightly, and felt beads of sweat gather on her face.

'O darling of Thebes.' She took the words from Abu Samil. 'Sit in peace, with thy face turned towards the north wind, and thine eyes filled with love.'

Abu Samil and Mike stared at her.

'You know this?' Abu Samil asked. 'How is this so?'

All Rosanna knew was that, even though the bowl had somehow ended up in the Tutankhamun collection, it had nothing to do with him. The message belonged to another.

'I don't know. It was just something ...' she faltered. 'That phrase was suddenly familiar to me. It was as if — I can't explain ...'

Rosanna shook her head. She did not know what was happening to her. Her heart had become so heavy, so overwhelmingly sad.

There was something just beyond her consciousness, something of infinite melancholy, that she couldn't quite reach. Where had those words come from? How had she known them? And why was she filled with such a terrible ache of emptiness?

Chapter Five

Rosanna sat on her bed, swathed in scarlet and gold. Coming away from the Museum her depression had lifted, and they had spent a pleasant afternoon exploring Gezirah Island and taking the lift up to the twenty-sixth floor of the Cairo Tower to admire the view. On a clear day, they were told, you could see the pyramids away to the south. Unfortunately, on that afternoon the heat haze had deprived them of that first glimpse, but at least they could gaze down at the city sprawled below, baking in its pall of dust, with the silver gleam of the river drawing the eyes away to the hills. They had returned to the hotel to freshen up before dinner.

There was a knock at the door. 'Are you decent?' a male voice shouted. It made Rosanna jump.

'Is that you, Mike?'

'Of course it is,' the cheerful voice replied. 'Who were you expecting? O'Neill?'

'Don't be silly. '

'Well, are you going to let me in, or have I got to stand here bawling all night?'

Rosanna opened the door and Mike, clad in an immaculate white tuxedo and an open-necked black silk shirt, slipped swiftly into her room. 'Shh.'

'What on earth are you doing?'

His ear was bent to the door, and after a moment he carefully wrapped his hand around the handle, pulled it open and leapt outside. Seeing no one, he grinned sheepishly and came back into the room.

'Will you please tell me what's going on?'

'I've been followed,' he declared, turning towards Rosanna at last. It gave her immense gratification to see the way his expression changed. Her efforts of the last half-hour had not been wasted. She had thrown a transparent Indian cotton evening dress over a white silky polo-neck shirt and white silk trousers. Mike gave a low, sexy whistle.

'Like it?' she said sweetly, doing a twirl. The glittering gold and scarlet threads spun out like a gossamer web.

'You're a sensation, Rosie!' He took a step nearer.

'You're rather magnificent yourself,' Rosanna said, thinking that he was far too handsome for his own good. 'What do you mean — followed?' She rummaged on the dressing table for her earrings. Mike plonked himself without ceremony on the bed.

'I was followed,' he said. 'An Egyptian. The Prof told me I wouldn't be able to get any more film after we left Cairo until we hit civilisation again at Luxor, so I thought I would nip out and get a couple more rolls, just to be on the safe side. As soon as I left the hotel this chap began creeping along behind me. Every time I stopped, he kept trying to touch me. I thought he was just after baksheesh, so I ignored him. I walked for miles looking for the bloody film, and never lost this geezer once. He tailed me the whole way.'

'Did he come back into the hotel behind you?'

'I'm not sure. I came breezing in and charged up the stairs without waiting for the lift. I'm on the fourth floor, you know. Then I locked myself in my room and got changed, and I haven't seen him since. But it's weird, isn't it? What do you think he was after? My body? Or my camera?'

Rosanna shrugged. 'I wouldn't leave either lying around,' she said. In the mirror, she saw Mike come up behind her. His beautiful dark eyes were trying to trap hers. She dared not look at him.

'Sorry to keep you waiting,' she mumbled. 'It's heat fatigue. My fingers are slippery, and my brain won't work properly.'

'What are you trying to do?' His arm snaked round her waist.

'Just fix this earring.'

'You've got earrings on already,' he murmured.

'I've had my ears pierced twice.'

'Are you kidding?'

'It's fashionable in England.'

Mike took hold of a handful of her hair and swept it out of the way so that he could examine her ear.

'You're not kidding.' He turned her round to face him. Rosanna felt she was rapidly getting out of her depth. 'I sure as hell want to kiss you, Rosie,' he said. 'How about it, sweetheart?'

'I never kiss Australians on an empty stomach,' she said, pulling away. 'Far too dangerous.' That made him chuckle. But it was a deep, throaty chuckle, as if he were the wolf sitting up in bed dressed as Grandma, and she had just tiptoed into the cottage with her basket of goodies. My, what big eyes he had.

He had put his arms round her again.

'Do you realise,' he whispered, nuzzling his nose against her neck, 'that the rest of the gang will be halfway through their meal by now?'

'Then you'd better stop bothering me, and let me finish!' she said, weakly.

He let her go, moved to the door, and leaned against it whistling. Thankfully, her earring slipped into place without more ado, and she grabbed her shawl and her bag, and was ready.

Mike was right. The rest of the party looked up accusingly as they made their entrance. They had to run the gauntlet of raised eyebrows, and to Rosanna's dismay the seats had been taken in such a way that she was obliged to sit next to O'Neill, while Mike joined the Professor and Joey and the Springer girls at the far end of the table.

It was not until the second course was served that O'Neill condescended to acknowledge Rosanna's existence. But when he did, she was pleasantly surprised to discover that he was prepared to be friendly.

'You made quite an impression on Abu Samil today,' he said, offering her what was left of the platter of spiced aubergines.

'Is he going to be our regular guide?' she asked.

'Depends. They're a funny lot, are Egyptian guides. Usually they all have their own little patches of territory, which they defend viciously. But sometimes you can get one to accompany you on a complete trip. It's expensive, but it's probably cheaper, in the long run, than forking out baksheesh for all the others en route. At any rate, Abu Samil was very taken with you.'

Rosanna laughed.

'I thought I was just being a nuisance, Mr O'Neill.'

'Forget it. And please stop calling me "Mr O'Neill". The name's Finbar. Listen, tiredness and heat affect people in different ways. They make you feel shaky, and they make me bad-tempered. That's how it goes. Nobody's perfect.'

Rosanna wondered if her ears were playing tricks on her. She glanced up at Finbar, who was innocently chewing away. He certainly seemed much less formidable now.

'You don't like Abu Samil very much, do you?' she asked.

'Not much, but I've invited him across for a drink. Might as well make the effort of getting to know him. Perhaps you'd like to stick around. Then you can chat to him as much as you like about your beloved Rameses.'

'Don't call him that!' Rosanna shuddered, recalling the statue's haughty face. 'I have a built-in hatred for that guy.'

'Oh yes, I forgot. Poor old Rameses — I wonder what he ever did to earn all this dislike from our Miss March.'

'I think Miss March has had enough for one day,' Rosanna

said, evading his question. 'I intend to have an early night, to catch up on my sleep.'

'And disappoint your boyfriend?'

Finbar's eyes pointed down the table to Mike, who had his head thrown back in laughter at some witty remark Jean Springer had made. She was gazing at him, her eyes glittering. Rosanna nearly choked on her mouthful.

'I beg your pardon?'

'I noticed you come down with young Cooper. Sorry our seating arrangements spoiled all your fun. Do you see him scowling away down there? He's been seething with frustrated lust throughout the meal.'

'I think, Mr O'Neill,' Rosanna said frostily, 'that my friendship with Mike is none of your business.'

Finbar shrugged, and stared at the fiery blush that spread from her cheeks to her neck.

'It's all part of being a courier and keeping an eye on you kids. I soon work out who's teaming up with whom.'

'You can be too clever, it seems.'

'Just as well. I want you up at five tomorrow.'

'Five?'

'I'm serious. We'll be on the road by six. That way we should avoid the worst of the traffic, and we'll get to the pyramids before the Americans do.'

'Does that make any difference?'

'I'll say.' He broke off their conversation to inform everyone else of the early start.

'Dawn in the desert,' Rosanna said dreamily. 'I can't wait.'

'It's not as romantic as it sounds,' Finbar told her.

They finished the meal with a small helping of delicate pink jelly, and then adjourned to the terrace. A cool breeze shifted the hanging dust of the day. Cairo was a blaze of orange lights under a mass of stars.

Chapter Six

'The interesting thing about disease,' confided Professor Bloxham, ramming Egyptian tobacco into his battered pipe with an equally battered forefinger, 'is to trace its history, its evolution. That's where one can really make discoveries nowadays. Never mind all the tramping through rain-forests and getting covered in leeches. I leave all that sort of thing to the young and innocent. What I like is a good, clean mummy to get my teeth into, then I'm as happy as a lark.'

'Really?' Two smoke rings curled skywards as Jean Springer tapped her cheek with a long scarlet nail. They were seated at a small table on the terrace, the Professor presiding over a bottle of Greek brandy. Mike had gone to the bar in search of something to go with it.

'Guts and stomachs happen to be my bread and butter,' he beamed, 'particularly the remains of the fascinating little chaps that burrow their way into them.'

'Anything guaranteed to turn your own,' groaned Jean.

Rosanna was grateful that this subject had not gripped the party at the table earlier.

In the 70s, Professor Bloxham informed them, he had been given a grant by the Smithsonian and sent to Egypt to supervise arrangements for the autopsy of a large number of mummies, and to obtain facts to back up his theories.

Rosanna did not approve. Those grisly remains had all been living beings once, somebody's aunt, or brother, or grandfather. She was glad that they hadn't seen the royal mummies in the Museum, and she could understand the feelings of the Egyptians who were campaigning for their reburial. After all, she did not imagine many English people would be too thrilled at the idea of a boat-load of Egyptians arriving to dig up Queen Victoria and make a sideshow of her naked body.

'What about treasure?' interrupted Joey. 'I bet you must have picked up loads of loot during your travels.'

'Jewels buried in the wrappings —' Jean's face took on a dreamy look. 'Gold —'

Finbar's ears pricked up. 'Listen, all of you, don't you know this sort of talk is dangerous? Unless you really fancy rotting for a couple of years in a stinking prison cell.'

'They wouldn't lock *Jean* up!' declared Bertice, tossing her head. 'They wouldn't dare!'

'They'd save her for a fate worse than death, I would imagine,' Finbar drawled, rather spitefully. 'Or chain her to a wall and toss away the key. While you're with me, Miss Springer, you will not mess about. Is that clear? I can assure you I've had my own little moments with the Egyptian police, and I'm not looking for any more trouble.'

'Hey! This is our first real night. We're all far too serious!' complained Bertice. 'I think we should have a party. In our room — everyone welcome.' She jiggled about in imitation of an oriental dancer.

'I'm sorry, girls, but you'll have to count me out,' Finbar dismissed the idea. 'I've got paperwork to do, and business with Abu Samil. Maybe another night.'

'Me too,' said Rosanna. 'Don't you realise, this monster said five o'clock!'

'So he wants us up at five!' Bertice was scornful. 'The night is young, and I'm in the mood.'

'I'll come,' Joey said excitedly.

Bertice groaned. 'Oh, God — who asked *you*? We want to enjoy ourselves, not babysit!'

Rosanna left the balcony just as Mike came back with a trayful of Cokes.

'You're not leaving us?' he asked, surprised and disappointed.

'Sorry. I'll feel more like living it up tomorrow,' she promised. 'You're not short of admirers, Mike. Go and make the other girls happy.'

'I'll give you until tomorrow — then I'm coming to get you!'

'My, my, Grandmother — what big teeth you have!' Rosanna laughed, and headed off to her room.

* * *

I'm late. I hurry along the path through the cane-brakes, praying that he has not given up and gone away. Over my head the sky is filled with sun, sun striking the land with arrogant and overwhelming force. The oxen are dozing in the shade of trees. I am going as fast as I can, but the sun is watching for any movement on the parched land, and its arrows of heat strike at me. In the canes, something has frightened the wild ducks and they rise whirring into the sky.

He has to be there still, waiting for me, his strong arms eager to hold me close against him in the tall shade of the papyrus beds. My lips are salty from the sweat of hurrying. Why will my legs not bear me faster to my beloved? It is my only chance to come today, now in the hour when the workers are resting. Only a little further ...

Praise the gods, he is there! There in the papyrus beds I see a man, tall and bronzed, the man my soul adores. I risk calling to him.

'You see, my love! I did not fail. I have come to you, as I promised.'

He turns to meet my radiant smile, my joy at finding him.

But it is not him. It is not my lover who comes smiling towards me, his arms outstretched to hold me, his eyes filled with triumph. My heart beats so furiously that my voice is shaking as I cry out: 'Where is he? What have you done with him?'

'Don't be foolish!' He seizes my wrist, jerks me towards him.

40

I fall against this man's cold heart, seeing the cruel sneer twist his lips. 'Did you think I would let him steal what is mine, steal you from under my nose?'

'I will never be yours!' I scream at him. 'You will never use me!'

Somehow I find the strength to tear my wrist from his grasp, push him away. The cane-brake sways and hisses as I hurl myself through it. I must find my prince, find him and warn him ... Or is it already too late?

The world is going black with a great despair.

* * *

Rosanna woke up with a start, the dream still vivid in her mind. Her body was soaked with perspiration. She clicked on the lamp. It was only two o'clock. Had she slept at all?

It was hot and stuffy in her room. She got up and padded to her little bathroom, where the air was even more hot and humid. It was stifling. No wonder she couldn't sleep.

She stripped off her nightdress and hung it from the hook. Hopefully, she rattled the handle of the shower, but was granted nothing more than a meagre trickle of cold water. She stood there cooling off for a couple of minutes, then turned the drips off and reached for the towel.

There was a click. Rosanna froze. It had sounded exactly as if someone had just closed her door. She stood very still, listening.

Suddenly the water-pipe gave a gurgle, making her jump and nearly slip on the wet tiles. She gripped the towel tightly and listened again.

Nothing. Hotels in Cairo were bound to be full of clicks and raps and strange noises, things that went bump in the night. Why, her own shower struggling to perform must have disturbed the people in the adjacent rooms. She flung the towel over her shoulder and began to dry her back.

There was another click. And a scuffle. Three seconds of silence, then the scuffle again. Rosanna stood stock still, not daring to go out of the cubicle to look.

Somebody breathed heavily through his nose. Rosanna's knuckles were white with tension. Someone had got in, and that person must have a key, since she was certain she had locked the door.

Her ears strained against the silence. She wished she could see what the thief was doing. Suppose the man discovered her in the shower? He obviously could not have realised she was there. Yet he could surely see that the bed was empty.

Rosanna realised, with a shudder of enlightenment, that the intruder might have known about the Springer girls' party, and assumed that she was there — if it was still going on. The thought flashed across her mind that the intruder might possibly be O'Neill; but what happened next ruled that theory out.

A deep, guttural voice began to intone what Rosanna could only assume was a religious chant. Three times the same sonorous phrase was repeated; then there was a pause; and then another phrase was softly repeated for a few seconds. Then the intruder, obviously quite unaware that he was not alone in the room — for he made no further attempt to muffle his footsteps — began to walk towards the shower cubicle.

Here it comes, Rosanna thought, wrapping the towel firmly around her body and tucking the ends in tightly across her bosom. She looked round for anything she might use as a weapon. There was nothing, not so much as a bath-brush.

Faint with fear, she stepped back silently into the small space beside the toilet, and pressed herself against the wall. She hoped that if he didn't look too carefully, since he was not expecting to see anyone, the small folds of the shower curtain might be enough to hide her. She froze, waiting.

The footsteps stopped at the cubicle. Then — a detail Rosanna might have found comical but for the circumstances — a hand appeared and went for the light switch.

That was all he was doing, just turning out the light. A conscientious thief, this. It convinced her even more that it must be one of the hotel staff. Who else would do such a thing?

The cubicle was plunged into darkness, but not before Rosanna had taken note of a thin brown arm in a blue cotton djellaba. Abu Samil? Surely not! He had been wearing a djellaba like that — but then, didn't everybody in Egypt? On the middle finger of the hand she had seen a large gold ring with a square black stone.

The intruder quickly opened the outer door and went out. Rosanna waited a moment in case he returned, then stumbled out of the cubicle, put on her nightdress, and switched on the light again. What had he taken? She looked round the room. Nothing seemed to have been disturbed. The things she had placed out on the dressing-table were all untouched.

She wrenched open the table drawer. Relief flooded through her when she saw her leather wallet, also apparently untouched. She picked it up gratefully and checked its contents. Passport, documents, traveller's cheques — everything was in order. Rosanna could not believe her luck. She felt almost sorry for the thief who had missed what he must have come for. It was too good to be true.

She pulled her case out from under the bed and opened the lid. Yes, there were small signs that it had been rifled; and yet she could find nothing missing.

In the bottom left-hand corner, however, something caught her eye. Something that had not been there before.

Rosanna reached down and picked it up, and held it in her hand wonderingly. It seemed that the 'thief' had taken nothing after all, but on the contrary had left her a present. She gazed, enthralled, at an exquisite statuette, an inch in height, glowing golden in the artificial light. Two round, savage eyes gazed back at her over an imperious beak. It was Horus, the Hawk God.

Chapter Seven

The minibus approached those ancient wonders of the world before which, according to the *son-et-lumière* brochure, no man could stand without gasping in awe. Abu Samil stood up in the bus, and turned towards the pyramids and the rising sun.

Rosanna clutched the golden hawk. The savage little beak dug sharply into her hand. Horus, the divine son of Osiris, had done little to reawaken in her any enthusiasm for early morning adventures. The call at five o'clock — waking her abruptly from the fitful sleep into which she had at last subsided — followed by a zombie-like wash and breakfast before they were bundled out onto the street, had given her no opportunity to report the intruder in her room. They had been out on the road while her mind was still struggling to wake up. So she had told no one.

'I hear you ask, my dear young friends,' Abu Samil, began after clearing his throat noisily, 'I hear you ask yourselves — what is a pyramid? What is the meaning of these huge piles of stone that challenge the sky and raise our eyes from earth to heaven?'

'Did you ask that?' whispered Joey, grinning behind his guidebook so that Abu Samil could not see his face.

'Behold!' he commanded, as the bus bounced to a halt in a rock-strewn car-park, narrowly missing a couple of rather moth-eaten camels. 'See here the pyramids whose very names are famous throughout the world — "Great is

Chephren", "Horizon of Khufu", "Divine is Menkaure".'

'As every schoolboy knows,' commented Jean Springer tartly. Abu Samil ignored her.

Rosanna, now that she was awake, was beginning to wonder what on earth she was going to do about the golden hawk, and whether or not she ought to get it over with by reporting the whole matter to O'Neill.

She sneaked another glance at the statuette, carefully cupping it in her hands so that no one else would see. Horus, son of the god, symbol of the surging force of life.

Osiris the Good, king of the gods, had an evil brother who was overcome with bitter jealousy. This brother, Set, created a wonderful coffin and persuaded Osiris — who was incapable of evil thought and therefore suspected nothing — to try it out for size. Instantly Set nailed it shut, heaved it to the Nile, and drowned him.

However, their sister Isis, who was married to Osiris, was determined to search for the missing body. Eventually she found the coffin far away in the land of Phoenicia, enclosed in the bark of a tamarisk tree. Not being Queen of Magic for nothing, she fanned sufficient life back into her husband-brother's corpse for him to lie with her and impregnate her with Horus, their son.

But Set was bound by his inexorable hatred and could not accept the defeat, and Osiris was bound by his immortal innocence and trust. So Set successfully killed his brother a second time, hacking him to pieces and scattering the sacred limbs.

Once again Isis was thrown into an agony of grief and made a painstaking search for the remains of her unfortunate beloved. She managed to locate every part of him — except one. That one significant piece which had made him Lord of Life, the sacred phallus, had been tossed into the Nile and eaten by a fish; so all power of life and creativity now depended on the god-child, Horus of the Dawn, who was destined to grow up and take revenge upon his evil uncle. The various remains of Osiris were buried where Isis found them, and his soul departed to become Lord of the West.

Rosanna folded the figurine back in its paper napkin and tucked it away carefully in the depths of her shoulder-bag. This was not the time or place to worry about it.

They were out of the bus and into the fresh air of early morning. Finbar noted with satisfaction that there were no other vehicles in the car-park. He negotiated quickly with the guardians of the site and handed out tickets, advising those who wanted to go inside the pyramid to do this before they did anything else.

'There's the boat-pit,' he told them, 'and the whole area round the Sphinx. If you want to go inside the smaller pyramids they'll let you, if you fork out backhanders. But if you take my advice, you'll finish with Divine Khufu before the Mongol hordes arrive. It gets very cramped in the passageways, and there's not much air in there. Don't go in at all if you're claustrophobic! Anyway, I certainly don't intend to carry anyone out!'

'Gee, thanks!'

And there it was: after all those films and books and magazines that had made it familiar to the whole world, the real thing was staring them in the face, seeming to increase in size with every step they took towards it.

'Are you going inside, Rosie?' said Joey, bouncing along at Rosanna's elbow. 'You're not claustrophobic, are you?'

'Try and stop me! Getting to the King's Chamber has been one of my life's ambitions. And afterwards, I'm going to climb up the outside to the top!'

'Just a minute!' Rosanna hadn't realised that Finbar had come up behind them. 'You can forget that idea. That climb is off. Strictly out of bounds.'

'But everybody does it. My grandfather did it! There's a book at the top started by Mark Twain that everyone signs!'

'Forget it. Like I told you, it's out of bounds to tourists now.'

46

'But why?'

'Too many accidents.'

'I wouldn't fall! I must go up. It's one of the reasons I came. It's something I simply have to do.' Rosanna was nearly in tears.

She knew she could do it. Climbing the towering mass would certainly be strenuous, and would probably be ill-advised later in the day, but it was not all that hot as yet; it was the perfect time.

'For God's sake, Rosie, do as you're told, will you? It's dangerous, and in any case, it's illegal now. The guards wouldn't let you go up.'

'What guards?'

Finbar pointed to the skyline along the angle of the pyramid. A minute blob of white, some three-quarters of the way up, obligingly stood up and was silhouetted briefly against the sky before disappearing round the shoulder of the rocks.

'Those guards.' Finbar stalked off towards the entrance. Rosanna's resistance crumpled. She could have sat down and cried. Wretched with disappointment, she plodded across the sand.

Looking up, she saw Abu Samil sitting grandly by a dark hole, some fifty feet above ground level, as if he owned it.

Maybe she could talk to him? He didn't make her feel small and stupid. Maybe she would even tell him about her dreams, if the right moment cropped up.

She waved to him, and he climbed down to meet her.

'Come now, Miss Rose,' he chided. 'You are hesitating?'

Rosanna took the opportunity to snatch a glance down at his hand, to see if he wore a gold ring with a black stone. His leathery brown arm had a better-fed appearance than the one which had reached for her light switch, and there was no ring.

Now that she stood against the actual building blocks of the pyramid, Rosanna realised that they were big — much bigger than they had appeared from a distance. She had read that if the blocks were all dismantled again, they would form a wall ten feet high around the whole of France. Along one ledge three black goats were ambling nonchalantly in the sun. Their amber eyes looked her over dubiously.

Abu Samil began to help her climb up to the entrance, showing her where to place her feet. He held out his hand. It would have been churlish to refuse his help. Rosanna placed her palm in his and, feeling like a toddler trailing behind a fussy mother, allowed him to pull her up the track.

They had to duck their heads to enter the hole, and in an instant the light of day was cut off and they were plunged into sepulchral gloom. A corridor dropped down sharply in front of them; Rosanna knew it would rise later, in a long, low passage and then a high one leading up to the King's Chamber. There were electric light bulbs, providing a dull glimmer, and Abu Samil had a torch which he shone on the ground to be on the safe side. Rosanna touched the solid bulk of the enclosing carved blocks and shivered.

This was the moment when all claustrophobics realised that their ambitions had been greater than their good sense. She put out her hand to steady herself. Millions of tons pressed down upon her.

Abu Samil's fingers closed softly around her arm. He was so quick to react that Rosanna knew he must have been waiting for her hesitation. It did nothing to reassure her.

'Not frightened, Miss March?' he smiled.

'A little,' she admitted. She took a deep breath, then crouched over and began the long ascent.

By the time they emerged into the high vaulted passage that ended in a granite antechamber, Rosanna's back and thighs were aching. It was sheer bliss to stand upright again and have a stretch. She was forced to admit, grudgingly, that Finbar had been right: the climb would have been considerably more unpleasant if they had been wedged in a crowd, unable to breathe.

She closed her eyes, savouring the moment when she would see for herself, at last, the King's Chamber, one of the most famous rooms in all history. She gave her imagination full sway, thinking of the glittering jewels, the gleam of gold, the fabulous treasures and works of art that the Pharaoh would have had interred with him ...

Abu Samil drew her into the room.

'Come, my dear,' he said softly. 'You should open your eyes now.'

Rosanna found herself standing in a small, depressing place made entirely of black, highly-polished granite. The mammoth blocks were laid so close that you could not thrust a knife between them.

The only object in the room was the huge but simple sarcophagus hewn in dark pink granite, tarnished by millions of sweaty tourist hands. It was uninscribed, and without a lid, and on its rim — perched malevolently like some overgrown leprechaun, with his arms folded and his legs crossed — was the grinning figure of Finbar O'Neill.

'Finbar!'

'Who did you expect? Don't tell me — old Cheops himself?'

'What are you doing here?'

'Waiting for you.' Finbar's smile did not falter, but his voice was cold. 'Thought I'd let you keep the delectable Miss March all to yourself, did you, Abu Samil?'

Rosanna raised an eyebrow, and wondered at what stage she had become delectable. Abu Samil dropped her arm and leapt away from her side as if she had suddenly become red hot.

'Do not be absurd!' His face, by the murky light of the solitary electric bulb, had become ugly. Rosanna glowered at Finbar.

He slid down from the sarcophagus, allowing Rosanna to examine it more closely. He pointed out to her how it still bore the marks of the drill used by the ancient workmen.

One of the long sides had lost a large fragment.

'How did they pull it up here?' she wondered, thinking that there was no way a couple of thousand sweating, straining slaves could have fitted into the passage they had just ascended.

'People have suggested all kinds of pulley mechanisms, but the really odd fact is that this sarcophagus is actually *wider* than the passage.'

'That's impossible.'

'Not at all. It just means that it wasn't pulled up at all, but set in position here before the rest of the pyramid was built above it.'

'Oh.'

'Listen,' Finbar said. There was a large piece of timber lying in the corner. He picked it up with both hands and swung it at the empty sarcophagus. It rang like a bell, the sound reverberating and booming through the stones. He did it again, and laughed.

'That should send a few bats flying!'

'For heaven's sake — you should have more respect!' Rosanna chided him. 'Think of the poor ghosts.'

'Ah, ghosts!' chuckled O'Neill. 'Yes. Egypt is the most terrible place in all the world for them. You couldn't stir a foot in the old days for tripping over a ghost or a jinn!'

Rosanna knew he was teasing her, but the pyramid, after all, reared up in the midst of a vast necropolis. They were probably surrounded by more ancient mouldering corpses here than anywhere in the world. The very thought of being surrounded by so many dead made her shiver.

'There are no ghosts here,' Abu Samil reassured her. 'The ka of this pharaoh has long since risen and gone. The dead need their gifts and sacrifices if they are to survive.'

'I thought the pharaohs didn't believe that death separated the spirit from the body,' Rosanna said. 'Didn't they believe that the soul only went away for a little while?'

Abu Samil looked up, his eyes glistening. 'My dear,

50

simply to speak the names of the dead is to make them live again,' he said softly. 'It restores the breath of life to him who has vanished.'

'Then don't get me talking about Rameses,' Rosanna giggled nervously. Abu Samil stiffened. She realised that her frivolous remark was out of place.

'So long as the link is not broken,' cut in Finbar, 'the image not shattered, the false door not closed, and the body not destroyed for ever.'

'But now there are no more pharaohs. The tombs are empty, and the Egyptian gods are dead.'

Loud American voices, and a woman's laughter, could be heard wafting up the ascent. Finbar swore, and Abu Samil spat.

They burst noisily into the black chamber.

'Will ya look at this?' A middle-aged woman with grey hair dyed blue plucked at the sleeve of her owl-faced son.

'So what?' the boy whined. 'It's no big deal. I got dust in my throat. Gimme a Coke, will ya?'

'You the guide?' asked a man with big red lips that competed with the sunset scenes on his shirt. He poked a finger at Abu Samil.

'Your pardon, sir.' Abu Samil bowed and touched his finger to his heart. 'No speak American.' He bowed again and left the chamber. Rosanna and Finbar followed, suppressing their smiles.

Chapter Eight

Rosanna stretched herself out on the deckchair, enjoying the undivided attention of at least six waiters. On a wicker table at her right hand she had everything her heart desired — pitta bread and cream cheese, a glass of sweet hibiscus tea, and a little dish of expensive ice cream.

She turned over in her mind the strange business of the previous night. By now, of course, she should have reported the matter and handed over the hawk. She had told herself a hundred times that she was being extremely foolish to keep it.

There was a splash in the pool behind her, and droplets of cold water spattered onto her shoulders. A lean, dripping figure heaved himself up the ladder and stood in her sun. She lifted her head and glared at him.

'I suppose you couldn't shift a few inches to the right?' she asked coldly.

Finbar threw himself onto the adjacent deckchair. 'Give us a sip of your tea,' he said, unruffled by her hostility.

Rosanna manoeuvred into a sitting position and favoured him with a frosty stare. His torso was brown and magnificent. He lay back and cupped his hands behind his head, his bare brown feet protruding over the end of the chair.

'And how's my little friend today?' he asked, ignoring Rosanna's silence. She raised an eyebrow.

'Perfectly well, thank you for inquiring.'

'Oh, jolly good. Perfectly well.' He mimicked her voice, managing to make her sound like a spoilt member of the jet-set.

'Stop it, Finbar.'

He opened one eye, surprised by her vehemence, then closed it again.

'Climb down, princess,' he murmured. 'The weather's too hot for your tantrums.'

Abu Samil appeared in the doorway and saw them. It *was* a hot day. He was fanning his moustaches with a small woven papyrus mat.

'I hope you have forgiven my little outburst yesterday,' he said, addressing Rosanna as if Finbar did not exist. A click of his fingers brought one of the waiters scurrying up, and he ordered more ice cream.

'Of course. I was sorry we were interrupted. I was very interested in what we were discussing.'

'Ah. The ka,' he said. 'The eternal life-force of kings.'

'And you mentioned a false door, Finbar,' Rosanna said. 'I didn't understand what you meant by that. You said it was never to be closed.'

'Something our little expert doesn't know?'

'The tombs had two sections,' explained Abu Samil. 'The "dead" side, where the body was laid, and the "living" side, the *serdab* where the mourners could congregate. Between these two was a false door, carved in stone, dividing the mortal from the spiritual.'

'Each Osiris-king had a statue of himself placed in the *serdab*,' said Finbar, 'gazing out across the desert to the rising sun. The priests would come there every day and treat it as if it was the king himself. They would cleanse it, touch its mouth with the holy adze and chisel and rub it with milk, making it ready to receive the dead king's ka when it wished to glide through from the other side.'

'What?'

'It would come through the door.'

For once Abu Samil was completely in tune with Finbar. 'Every day the ka would come and feed at his altar, and claim the gifts that gave him strength,' he said. 'There the priests kept him alive and waiting.'

'Alive? Oh, come on ...'

There was a flush of sweat making Abu Samil's face shine.

'Any soul could come back to the body and re-enter the world of the living,' said Finbar, 'so long as the body was well preserved. Obviously, once the body was allowed to rot away, the soul could never use it again. That's why the royal Egyptians went to all that bother to preserve their corpses. If the corpse went, the soul could no longer get back to earth.'

'However, the ka of Horus is far too important to depend on grieving relatives keeping corpses preserved,' murmured Abu Samil. Finbar raised an eyebrow. 'A cadaver is just a shell, after all, which gets laid aside. The god-ka makes use of other settling-places — anything it can recognise and enter.'

Rosanna began to feel uneasy, thinking of the statue in her bag.

'What sort of settling-places?'

'Anything that was connected with him personally, or that he could recognise because it bore his likeness or his name,' said Abu Samil. 'A statue, a painting, a locket perhaps. Those who loved and honoured him would have some small amulet, in their rooms or worn among their jewellery, that he could use.'

'And that would mean that he could actually come into their rooms? Be with them?'

'Of course. And commune with them, if they were sensitive.'

'Did they really believe that?'

'Why not?' said Finbar. 'It's not very different from modern spiritualism.'

This was the moment when Rosanna should have told him about the statue, but she clamped her lips tight. Some intuition prevented her.

'And that is why,' Abu Samil continued, 'the hardest punishment for failed princes was to break their statues, erase their names, and chip them off their monuments. The dead ones then had no way to return to this world; they became nothing, and simply fell into the great void.'

'They did that to Tutankhamun, didn't they?'

'They tried. Yes, there was a systematic attempt after his death to wipe him utterly from history.'

'It's hard to understand such a ruthless hatred.'

Finbar grinned. 'Don't worry,' he said. 'It's harder than you think to kill a god forever.'

'Whether or not Tutankhamun still exists,' Abu Samil said softly, 'I cannot say. Yet he, too, once bore the name of Horus.'

'Why did you speak of Horus?' Rosanna's pulse quickened. It was Finbar who answered, however.

'Horus is Lord of the Rising Sun,' he murmured, so quietly as to be almost speaking to himself. 'Born of the sky, the new life from Osiris who died that the divine race might perpetuate itself. He breathes again through the bodies of his offspring, the sons of the Sun. All Osiris-pharaohs, when they come to life again, become Horus.'

Suddenly Rosanna became afraid even to think of the golden hawk that nestled, wrapped in its humble paper napkin, in the depths of her bag. The little statue seemed to weigh a million tons; she felt that the golden materialisation was holding back a surge of inconceivable force.

'Very good, my friend.' Abu Samil's voice was a sneer of contempt. 'Soon I will just take my pay and sit in your shadow.'

Rosanna shivered. The guide's sudden and unexpected hostility had the impact of cold water being rudely thrown over her. She was sure Abu Samil had done it deliberately

55

and maliciously, determined to spoil a moment that had stretched itself beyond time and reality.

He changed the subject. 'Did you read, by the way, of the new murder case under investigation? I hope it does not interfere with our intended stay in Karnak.'

Finbar was visibly irritated. 'I've read it,' he snapped, 'and I couldn't care less. Might I suggest, Abu Samil, that you go about your business and stop trying to frighten Miss March.'

'Miss March knows there is no such intention in my head, I am sure. But I am a busy man. I will go, if you insist.'

'I'm sure you have things to do. Don't let us keep you.'

Abu Samil bowed, and left them. Rosanna watched him go with mixed feelings. He walked like a crab — yes, just like a crab that had done damage and was looking for a rock to sidle under to gloat about it.

Finbar was flat on his back again, fumes of annoyance almost visible around him.

'Murder?' she probed.

'It's nothing to get alarmed about. Take no notice.'

'Then why did Abu Samil mention it?'

'He just wanted to stir us up. I'll give you the paper. You can read it all for yourself. A few people have gone missing during the last couple of years, gone without a trace. And there have been one or two rather strange killings. Now, apparently, a mutilated corpse has turned up buried in a field at Karnak.'

'Where we're going.'

'Yes. They say it looks like a ritual killing. Possible magical significance.'

'You're making fun of me, aren't you?'

'My dear Miss March, you are so delightfully innocent. We may be enjoying a private swimming pool in a Cairo hotel — but out there it's just the eternal sand and the eternal Nile, and the eternal fight for survival. If the blood of a virile man was used for thousands of years to guarantee a good Nile and a good harvest, try telling the modern fella-hin that such sacrifices aren't necessary now. Oh yes, they have the Dam and they have the Government, but they know a price still needs to be paid. Probably even more so, now that the Nile is dammed and not allowed to flood like it was before.'

Rosanna sipped what was left of her tea.

'Are you honestly trying to convince me that a man was recently sacrificed at Karnak to ensure a good crop?'

Suddenly Finbar laughed at her serious face. 'Oh, Rosie, I'm only teasing you. I guess someone got chewed up by a jackal. You ought to see your face!'

Rosanna leapt up in a fury and hit him with the cushion from her deckchair. In self-defence, he grabbed her arms and held her while she tried desperately to hit him again. His laughter echoed across the pool. Rosanna was appalled at the sight of two waiters grinning at the scene.

'What's the matter?' Finbar chuckled. 'Prefer young Mike, eh?'

She launched herself at him, but he laughed and ducked, and caught her up in his arms, her limbs flailing against his strength.

'Too hot-headed by far,' he said. 'Into the water, I think.'

'You wouldn't dare!' she shrieked.

He carried her the three paces, and dropped her into the pool.

Chapter Nine

After lunch, Rosanna found Joey in a grumpy mood.

'I don't want to rest,' he complained. 'And I don't want to be left with the girls either.'

'Where's Mike?'

'He's got fed up with me. I'm too young for him too, I suppose.'

'Don't be silly. What *would* you like to do?'

'Take a look round the bazaar, I guess.'

'Let's go together,' Rosanna suggested, grabbing her bag.

A short taxi ride deposited them on the edge of the marketplace. It was very hot, and they took care to keep in the shade as much as possible, and do nothing more energetic than feast their eyes on the assortment of wares spilling out onto the streets.

Hefty black-veiled women swayed ponderously along, their plastic shopping bags bulging with grapes and cucumbers, aubergines and round flat bread. A flock of a dozen sheep edged through the crowd, bringing its own swarm of attendant flies. Their hooves slipped and clattered amongst the rubble, the broken Coca-Cola bottles.

After the glowing arcades of copper-workers, Rosanna and Joey headed into a section specialising in fabrics. Bales of rich materials were stacked up to eye level. Swathes of diaphanous silver-threaded chiffons and fine cottons trailed from overhead bars. Shopkeepers came bustling out to urge them into their caverns — 'Just for a look! No charge for looking!'

Joey tugged Rosanna's sleeve. 'Hey, Rosie — look!' She turned from a close inspection of a sad-looking bird trilling in a little cage.

'It's the Professor.'

'He hasn't seen us.'

'Let's follow him.'

They bobbed into the stream of people in his wake, but as suddenly as they had seen him he was swallowed up in the crowd. Rosanna pushed past a very corpulent man who had managed to get between them, and soon saw the floppy Panama hat again. She shouted, but the Professor didn't hear.

Taking a tight grip on her shoulder-bag, she plunged after him, determined not to lose him. Why on earth did the wretched man have to be in such a hurry? It was far too hot for such a ridiculous scramble. She shouted again, and it seemed that every single person in the market looked round except the man in the Panama hat. He obviously had other things on his mind.

Suddenly the Professor was no longer to be seen in the street, and neither was Joey.

'Oh no!' Rosanna stopped, bewildered, and gazed round. There was a small café to her left, full of semi-somnolent Cairenes sprawled in the shade, drinking tea — and, to her relief, there was the Professor just about to take a seat right at the back.

'Professor Bloxham!' she yelled. 'We've been chasing you for half a mile. And I've lost Joey!'

'Good lord, girl, you gave me a shock. What are you doing here?'

'Oh, we were just drifting about the market when we saw you. Joey's still out there somewhere.'

Rosanna realised he wasn't listening. He was looking past her, at a man in a short-sleeved khaki suit who was approaching their table. It was Hassan, whom they had met at the Museum. He had obviously expected to meet the Professor, and was surprised to find him in company.

Hassan reached the table and greeted the Professor with a motion that was half a bow and half a military salute. He said something in Arabic, and the Professor answered him. Both men then subjected Rosanna to a prolonged stare.

'Look, I didn't realise I would be in the way,' she muttered, feeling decidedly excess to requirements. 'If you'll excuse me, I'd better go and look for Joey.'

'No, no, my dear. Sit down. Sit down. Joey will be OK. He's an intelligent boy,' urged Professor Bloxham. 'You remember Miss March, of course,' he added to Hassan.

Hassan had not taken his eyes off her.

'I am charmed to meet you again,' he said. He had seemed perfectly affable before, but now, to Rosanna's dismay, he looked about as charming as a reptile about to make short work of a juicy beetle. He sat down and ordered Turkish coffee.

'Well, well, Professor,' he said eventually. 'I must say that this is a surprise.' He seemed amused by something.

The Professor, on the other hand, was not. 'You make too many assumptions, my friend,' he snapped. 'Far too many.'

'Ah. Things are never quite as they seem. I understand perfectly.'

'You understand nothing at all!' Bloxham had worked up quite a flush. He put a finger under his shirt collar and loosened it. 'Look here, have you any — er — business for me, or not? Just give me a straight answer, and don't play the fool.'

Hassan's eyes glittered. He ignored Bloxham and turned to Rosanna. An enormous smile did little to improve him.

'But — this young lady,' he said. 'What about this lady, Professor?'

'She has just found me by accident. You know very well

she's a member of the group.'

'But of course. A member of the group. You are a lucky man, Professor, to have such lovely members in your group. And so young and fresh ...'

'Hassan!' The Professor was really heated now. People were beginning to look. It was obvious Rosanna had stumbled into something he was extremely embarrassed about.

'And how do you like your group, Miss March?' inquired Hassan, still smiling. 'Is it a good group? A friendly one?'

'Yes, thank you. Very friendly.'

'Hassan — I haven't got time to waste!' Professor Bloxham cut in sharply. 'Have you anything you wish to discuss with me? In private, perhaps?'

The man was still smiling broadly. Bloxham was furious, and he was enjoying it. Rosanna wondered what on earth was going on.

'Not this time, Professor. Next time, perhaps.'

Bloxham pushed the table away from him as he stood up, making the little cups rattle.

'Thank you for nothing!' he snapped.

Hassan was not moved. 'Your time is so valuable,' he murmured. 'Even on this *holiday* tour.'

Rosanna began to feel that the Professor was in need of defence. There was nothing pleasant about Hassan.

'Excuse me, but the Professor's business is his own affair.'

'And you are just an English tourist eager to explore the bazaar. And pick yourself up a little treasure, perhaps?'

'Yes, indeed!' she laughed, attempting to lighten the conversation. 'A little treasure would come in very handy.'

'Then you must come with me, and see what I can show you, my dear.'

Hassan's hand closed over her arm, and she suddenly found herself being pushed towards a grey blanket that served as a curtain at the back of the café. The Professor stood by the table, his Panama hat clenched in one hand, doing nothing.

'Don't look so frightened,' Hassan said in her ear. 'I can offer you something much nicer than the usual tourist trinkets.'

The blanket was pulled back and Rosanna found herself in a small dark cubicle with a dirty table, two chairs, a lamp, and a rickety cupboard leaning against the wall.

Hassan was standing right behind her. She could feel his hot breath on her neck. The nerves in her stomach began to clench wildly with apprehension. She turned, just as he leaned forward to place his large hands on her shoulders. There was a ring with a black stone on his middle finger.

Stifling a scream, Rosanna stepped back and fell over one of the chairs. Hassan immediately bent forward to pull her to her feet.

'Don't touch me!' she yelled, her voice shrill in that confined space. 'Don't you dare touch me!'

He was breathing heavily. There was a leer on his hot face.

'Do not be silly, Miss March. Why should that old fool —'

'How dare you!' Rosanna's frightened voice verged on the edge of hysteria as she struggled free and stared desperately past Hassan at the thick grey curtain. He looked surprised. The smile faded at last, to be replaced by a perplexed frown.

'Miss March, please be calm. I assure you — I have no intention —'

'Let me out of here!' she insisted. 'I don't want your antiquities or treasures, or anything else to do with you!'

'I have no antiquities here,' he said quietly, almost apologetically. 'No real treasures. But you must surely have known that, Miss March. You must have —'

'Will you please stand aside and let me go!'

'Madam, wait. Please! I have made a mistake, that is all. I thought you — and the Professor with you — maybe Abu Samil —'

'Abu Samil?'

'It's nothing. Nothing.' Now an expression crossed his

face that might have been interpreted as fear.

'You are disgusting!' Rosanna realised he had no intention of moving, and she would have to push past him. 'Get out of my way!' She strode firmly towards the curtain, and to her great relief Hassan did not attempt to stop her.

Apparently the sudden thought that had occurred to him about Abu Samil had completely deflated him. Rosanna didn't stop to wonder why, or to consider the relationship between the two men. The only thing that mattered at that moment was to get out. She thrust herself past the curtain and back into the café.

It seemed bright now, after the murky shadows of that dreadful little room. Cairenes were sitting at their tables, smoking hookahs and drinking coffee, their eyes glazed with contented somnolence. The table at which she had sat with the Professor was occupied by two men in white djellabas. They were shuffling dominoes. There was no sign of the Professor.

He had gone, and left her there alone. Rosanna couldn't believe it. She took two paces forward. The proprietor, polishing glass cups behind the counter, looked at her blankly as if he had never seen her before. She glared at him furiously.

'Where is the man I was with?' she demanded.

The man shrugged. It was that huge, expressive Egyptian shrug.

'Who can say, madam?'

Hassan had followed her out. He was smiling again, his face all innocence, as if nothing whatever had happened. He looked so meek, so apologetically humble. God, Rosanna thought, was she going crazy? Was it all just her nerves? Had she, after all, simply misinterpreted everything that had just happened?

She glowered at Hassan. No, she had not. She knew it, and he knew it, but she had no witnesses, and the Professor had gone.

63

'Can you get me a taxi?' she demanded.

Hassan bowed. 'But of course. It is no problem. Leave it to me.'

He was as good as his word. In less than ten minutes a taxi had arrived and Rosanna was on her way back to the Hotel Hibis. It took somewhat longer before her heart ceased its wild racing, and the adrenalin stopped pumping.

* * *

At five o'clock there was a knock on her door.

'Who is it?'

'Me.'

'Oh, Joey!' Relief. Rosanna flung open the door and virtually dragged him inside. 'Am I glad to see you!'

'I thought you'd got fed up and dumped me deliberately.'

'It wasn't like that. Where's the Professor? Have you seen him?'

'He's gone shopping with the girls.' He sat down on her bed.

'Joey, there are things happening which are beginning to frighten me,' Rosanna said. 'I think I need help, but I don't know who to turn to. It all sounds so silly — but there really is something odd going on.'

Joey offered her a sweet. 'You really are upset, aren't you?'

Rosanna took a deep breath. 'I had rather a nasty experience this afternoon after I lost you. I found the Professor, but it turned out that he was meeting that man Hassan we saw at the museum — and, Joey — he was not a nice piece of work at all.'

'Yeah?'

She told him briefly.

'Joey, I was too scared to think. All I knew was that I had to get out of that room, and quick.'

'The point is — he was a friend of the Professor's, and the Professor just disappeared and left you in his clutches.'

'Exactly. He mentioned Abu Samil as well. And what I haven't told you is that there was another man sneaking about in my room last night.'

'Good grief, Rosie, you're popular!'

'It's not funny. It's all made me feel pretty insecure.'

'What happened?'

'I was in the shower. Someone came in, so I hid behind the curtain. All I saw was his hand. He had a black ring on. I thought he was a thief, but when he went there wasn't anything missing.'

'Maybe you shouldn't be on your own, Rosie,' Joey said gravely. 'Don't forget, Mike got pestered too.'

'And Joey, that Hassan was wearing one of those black rings too, the same as the man in my room.'

Joey took a long, sideways look at her.

'You do believe me, don't you? You don't think I'm making the whole thing up?'

'Oh, Rosie —'

'I'm not lying,' Rosanna said quietly. She opened her handbag and unwrapped the golden hawk. 'There you are.' She showed him triumphantly. 'That was left in my luggage by the intruder. He rummaged through my case, but didn't steal a thing. Then he sang some kind of weird hymn.'

'And left you a present.' Joey turned the hawk over and over in his hand. 'Horus.'

'Exactly,' she said. 'And that's only one of the odd things that have been happening to me. Ever since this holiday began something's been happening in my mind, and I'm quite sure that it has to do with Horus. Don't ask me what — I can't explain what I mean at all; but I keep getting vague memories of something that I can't quite remember, if you get what I mean. It's almost as if there's something trying to get through to me.'

'Well, at least this statue is solid, not just your imagination.'

'None of it's my imagination!' Rosanna retorted hotly.

'I'm frightened, Joey. There must be a reason for it.'

'I think,' said Joey slowly, 'that you should carry something to protect yourself with.'

'Good grief, I can't go traipsing about Egypt wielding a cleaver!'

'No, but you could carry a good-sized pocketknife. It would come in handy anyway when we go up-country — and it would certainly stop any troublemakers in their tracks.'

'Hmm.' She would have to think about that. She didn't want to end up with her throat cut by her own knife.

'Have you told Finbar?'

'Not yet. Can't you imagine how he'll react? He'll go mad because I didn't tell him straight away.'

Joey grinned. 'You're really in love with that guy, aren't you?'

'Oh, you've noticed! Yes, he and I were *born* for each other.'

Joey gave her back the hawk and she popped it back into her bag.

'Maybe you should tell him. He's supposed to be in charge of us.'

'Never mind him,' Rosanna said. 'I need information. I want to find out all there is to know about Horus. Have you got a book?'

'The Prof has. Or we could ask Abu Samil, if he comes across tonight.'

'No. Just for now, I'd rather keep him out of it.'

Chapter Ten

When Rosanna caught up with the Professor, he was poised with his backside hovering over the kind of soft canvas chair Rosanna associated with film producers. She bore down on him like a battleship with all guns primed. He hesitated in mid-air, taking in her furious expression, and decided to stand up rather than sit down.

'Professor Bloxham! I want a word with you.'

'Ah, there you are, my dear.' The Professor peered at her over his sunglasses. 'I've been waiting for you to come in. I've just had a phone call from Hassan. He was most concerned to ensure that you had arrived back safely at the hotel.'

'What?' She was all set to fire him down, but his air of utter innocence stopped her in her tracks.

'Yes. He seemed to be rather upset. I gather that you were under some kind of false impression about him.'

'Now, just a moment, Professor!' Rosanna was not mollified. 'When that wretched man dragged me through into that back room, you just cleared off and left me. Any reasonable person would have seen I was in an awkward situation.'

'Dragged you? I thought you were interested in his so-called souvenirs.'

'But you just left me there.'

'I think there has been a misunderstanding, my dear. I'm sorry. I'm afraid I didn't realise that you wanted me to stay with you. Put it down to my old bachelor ways. I

67

thought all modern young girls were quite independent these days, and able to cope. Most young women seem to positively resent interference.'

'You mean, you didn't think anything of leaving me with that man?'

'Good lord, no. Never entered my head.'

The Springer girls swept in at this point, magnificent in newly-acquired Egyptian dresses, to demand a little attention. They all went in to dinner.

During the meal Rosanna sounded the Professor out on the subject of Horus, and he promised he would indeed lend her a book.

'I hope it will make amends in a small way for my neglect of you this afternoon,' he said. 'I hope you have forgiven me?'

'Of course.' She hadn't really. Inwardly she was still fuming, but they were leaving Cairo the next day, and there seemed little point in keeping the argument going. And besides, she was very hopeful that something in the Professor's book might give her some clues to work on.

Later, the proud little statue, which Rosanna had ceremoniously placed in the centre of the dressing-table, watched her with gleaming eyes as she propped herself up on her pillows and flicked through page after page of details about ancient Egyptian history and religion.

She tried to concentrate, but the words were beginning to dance before her eyes, and soon she found that she kept dropping into sleep before she could reach the end of a paragraph.

Determined to keep going, she blinked furiously and re-read the section. Horus, Osiris, Isis, Set the Evil One ... Her mind filled with temples, huge palaces constructed for immortals a hundred feet in height.

* * *

There is no light in the temple except the silver moonlight. Its rays flood the ancient stones with a deathlike hue, and the cold light makes me tremble. I pull my cloak tightly round my shoulders. I have come to the solemn threshold forbidden to common mortals: the House of the Father.

Moonlight creeps through the arches and illuminates the far side of the great courtyard. The near side is a pattern of shadows, stretching out like fingers desperate to reach and grasp the protection of the altar.

I am not allowed to be here. I crouch low amongst the shadow of the stones and wait eagerly for the arrival of my beloved. Still he delays. If he does not come soon it will be dawn, and I will have to slip back to the palace before I am missed. Oh, Menkheperre, my love, why do you not hurry to be near me?

The stars are fading in the cold of dawn. Soon the sun will rise, glorious and demanding, the mighty Sun whom Menkheperre adores. The Sun — the Father, the Creator of Life, the God of the First Day, who opens his mouth to speak in the midst of silence. At the very mention of his name priests bow the head, and mortals prostrate themselves in the dust.

Menkheperre might have been a priest of the Sun, but he chose instead the path of a warrior. I am grateful for that, for the Sun-priests are never permitted to love a woman. Women belong to the Moon, the ruler of the night. The Moon can render a person unclean, and a priest of the Sun can have no contact with that which would make him weak or unclean. The Sun must triumph over all the evils of the night, or everything would weaken and die. Where would our life be without the Sun? He demands all the strength he can obtain.

I risk a great deal for my warrior. I have no right to be here. What would the priests say if they found a virgin girl in the temple? They would probably kill me.

The light is growing stronger. A bird flies across the courtyard; the whirr and beat of its wings startles the stillness. The glowing disc of the Sun, Horus Ra-Harakhte, begins to rise on falcon wings over the earth's rim. I ought to go now. I ought to creep away in the silence, while there is still time.

But the priests have purified themselves in the sacred pool, and come into the temple to kindle the fire, and fill their censers with charcoal and sweet-smelling resin.

They come to awaken the god, who still sleeps in his sealed tabernacle. They begin their chant, at first like the rustle of dry palm leaves, and then gaining in vigour as the Sun begins to rise and they approach the golden box in which his ka sleeps.

> *Awake, awake, O splendour of the Sun!*
> *Awake, awake, to the beauty of this new day!*
> *Awake in peace, O Lord of Karnak.*

I crouch low, shutting my eyes tight so that I will not see what I am not allowed to see. The song of the priests echoes among the huge columns. Where is my love? Why has he not come?

The High Priest enters, wearing his diadem, his purple robe spattered with droplets of pure gold. He cries out:

> *Awake, thou King of Heaven, ruler of the wide horizons.*
> *Gold of the dawn, we worship thee!*
> *See, the twin gates of heaven are opening.*
> *See, thy twin gates are swinging wide.*

The priest opens the door to the sacred image just as the sun's rays thrust over the horizon. The others lie on the ground in silence, their faces on the earth, their hands outstretched. With his golden adze, the High Priest touches the divine lips. Gently, he sprinkles the body of the god with water from four golden vessels and four which are red, the colour of life. The eyes of the god glow like golden fire. He can see me. I know that he can see me. I flatten myself against the flagstones, wet from the dew and the cold sweat of my body.

Forgive me, Lord, forgive me. You are the bringer of life and joy. You must understand, Lord, what it is to love. Menkheperre is your warrior, a hero in your service. How can you blame me for loving him?

The priests anoint the god, and dress him in new garments. They place in his gleaming hands the royal insignia, the flail and the crook.

'Horus! Horus!' they cry.

Thou bringer of life!
Though thou art far away, thy rays touch the earth!
Live, O Horus! For we live only through thee.

The priests bring forward a strong young man dressed only in a linen shift. His face is pale and drawn, but he steps proudly, like a king. He raises strong arms in a salute, arms that are beautiful and golden, anointed with oil. He stares straight into the eyes of the Sun. He does not fear. When he bows his head, it is the proud acknowledgement of one king to another.

The priest bows down before the young man, and puts his forehead on the earth. The young man stands proudly, still staring into the eyes of the god.

'Oh Horus,' he whispers, in a voice as gentle as a lover's, 'I give myself. Reply to me. Tell me, what is my duration of life with thee?'

The priest rises to face him.

'My son, thou art destined for millions of millions of years,' he says. 'A lifetime of millions.'

Another priest comes forward, holding a golden cleaver.

'Arise, O Avenger of thy Father! Rise with the dawn, thou great disc of the Sun.'

He bends towards the youth as if to kiss him. I hardly dare to breathe. The youth is gripped by the strong arms of four priests. His legs buckle, and the priests take his weight as he falls backwards. His head lolls. His eyes are open, but they no longer focus on this earth. They lay him on the great stone.

'Arise, O Sun, and give us life, as we give life to thee!'

The courtyard echoes with the song of the priests, the hissing of the sacred rattles, the beat of a large tambour. They turn the golden body so that his face presses on the slab. They stand in prayer, waiting to adore the Sun-boy's heart, the sacred blood given to the god.

Twelve priests approach the altar, bearing golden boxes. They bow, and raise the lids, to receive the severed limbs that will give life to the land.

Silence now, except for the solemn beat of the tambour. I bite my lip to keep back a scream. The High Priest takes the cleaver from his acolyte and raises it, gold and glittering, above his head.

* * *

Rosanna woke up with a start, the full blaze of the sun hammering on her face.

She sat up, in a state of some agitation, and stared round the room. Nothing had changed. The gilt cherubs, the white silk. Even the same three flies buzzing round the lampshade.

She gripped the sheets tight. This time she could remember every detail of her dream, and she realised, with a cold tremor of fear, that she had been the same girl, pining for the lover she could not find.

It was not just that she could not find him. She felt that something had happened to him, something terrible that was keeping him from her. She was quite sure that he could never willingly have put her through such torment. It had been more important to her than the fate of that sacrificed boy.

Rosanna slid out of bed and went to splash cold water on her face. The reflection that stared back at her looked quite shaken.

She knew his name now. That had come through quite clearly, and now it was in her conscious mind it was stuck there. Menkheperre — a warrior of the Sun.

And her love for him was dangerous. She knew, intuitively, that it offended the priests, and also the king. And

72

whoever offended the priests and the king was in grave peril.

Rosanna shook her head, tried to pull herself together. Then, with a great flood of relief, she realised that it was all O'Neill's fault. Of course! It was he who had filled her head with all those nasty thoughts about sacrifices. The things he had said had simply played upon her receptive mind.

She relaxed, and chided herself for her foolishness. And wait a minute — another flash of inspiration — the priest about to kill the boy with a cleaver ... Hadn't Joey said something about a cleaver, or a knife?

That was it. An amalgam of bits and pieces picked up by an overactive mind after all her upsetting experiences. Nothing more sinister than that. And she had probably triggered the whole thing by lying down where the sun shone on her face.

Rosanna grinned, glad that she had sorted it all out. Menkheperre, indeed. Some dream lover he'd turned out to be. Didn't even show up. She would take care not to dream about him again.

Chapter Eleven

The entire next day was spent travelling south.

Once away from the towns, they entered a world of brown and green that the centuries had scarcely touched. The mist stirred over the canals, revealing a jumble of squat mud-brick villages and the incredible order and neatness of the fields cherished by the fellahin. Little mud roads ran along above the level of the fields, where the owners of the richest soil in the world eked out their lives in poverty.

By the edge of the canals women did washing, naked boys swam, men transported their black soil in the same wicker baskets that could be seen in the wall-paintings of their ancient pharaohs. The tethered buffaloes cropped their circles through the deep clover, or plodded at the head of a small procession — the plough, the fellah and his sons, the neat white egrets stepping in the furrows.

The afternoon dragged by, field upon field, while the world slept. Through the valley moved the slow Nile, lapping reed banks, gliding past innumerable mud-flats. Swallows flicked the water, sun-bronzed men in loincloths stood in small rocking boats, casting their nets, sharp-winged white sails bleached in the fierce light. Rosanna closed her eyes and imagined hunting parties darting out on skiffs made of papyrus reeds, their boomerangs humming through the air, their cries scattering the teal into a clear sky, their cats crouched at the boat's edge eager to retrieve the stricken birds.

She pulled the little curtain to stop the afternoon sun from burning her right arm. In the bus heads were lolling, swaying from side to side with the motion of the vehicle. Mike Cooper sat propped cosily between the two Springer girls, asleep with a grin on his face, looking for all the world like a pasha in a harem.

At the front of the bus Finbar and the driver were the only ones awake. Once Finbar glanced up into the mirror, and caught Rosanna looking at him. She sank down immediately in her seat, but she knew that catching her out had given him malicious satisfaction.

At last the bus pulled into a tree-lined road alongside a railway station. At the outskirts of the town, where the houses petered out and the donkeys gathered at a forlorn ditch, the coach deposited itself with a triumphant shudder.

'You'll enjoy this!' announced Finbar, smiling malevolently at the glum faces of his charges, who were peering through the grime accumulated on the windows, eager to spot evidence of any sort of night life. There was none. The street was black, deserted but for a group of men squatting on the mud track, gently flicking the flies that landed on them with horse-tail switches. A solitary light bulb hung from a wire flung over a high wall, adjacent to a forbidding wooden gate. 'This is the best hotel in El Minya.'

The explorers climbed stiffly from the bus and stretched their weary limbs. A man came up to unleash the battered cases. This, then, was to be their home for the next two nights.

'Sorry, folks,' Finbar grinned blandly as he helped them down. 'No upmarket conditions here. I believe you were warned. We just have to make do as best we can.'

'Oh my God!' Bertice peered at the beaten earth street and the crumbling plaster on the walls.

'Brace up, girls,' said Mike. 'At least you'll be getting a little taste of the real Egypt.'

'A little taste of something, anyway!' groaned Jean, as a fly experimented with the sweat on her upper lip.

'I've had to put you in with the Springer girls here,' said Finbar to Rosanna. 'It'll be a bit of a push, I'm afraid, but it's the best I can do. Don't worry, it's only for a couple of nights.'

The girls were already in the room, fuming over the extra bed that left them barely enough room to walk about. There was a worrying display of splat-marks on the walls that indicated either spiders or cockroaches, and the only available toilet turned out to be a dilapidated communal affair down the corridor — but at least their room did have a shower unit that worked, and a plug-point hanging precariously from its wires in the wall.

Tea revived their spirits, and dinner — in the open air on the roof, as the sun set over the shadowy hills — was surprisingly good. As soon as the heat dropped after dark the town began to throng with people, and shops lit up and opened their doors for custom. The gang wanted to go out, but Rosanna had a fierce headache and a sore throat, and decided to beat a retreat.

She had just reached the door of the roof-garden when she realised that the person fumbling his way in was Finbar.

'Not going out with the others?'

'No. I — I thought —'

'Come and have a drink with me.' He took her arm, wheeled her smartly about, and steered her back to the tables. It was pitch dark now over Egypt; the last brilliant glow had faded over the Western Land, the Shore of the Dead.

Finbar plonked himself down opposite Rosanna and produced a couple of cans. A warm flush of pleasure coloured her cheeks. Why, she could almost believe he was pleased to see her. She rested her chin on her hands and gazed into his eyes boldly.

'Why don't you tell me about yourself, Mr O'Neill?' she asked. She said it very sweetly. He tapped her on the nose with one finger.

'Behave yourself, Miss March, or I will not be answerable for the consequences.'

'What consequences?'

'It may have escaped your notice, my child, but your friends have conveniently departed and left us alone.'

He put out his hand and covered hers. His fingers were slim, and warm, and muscular, and gentle. The shock of his touch electrified her. She snatched her hand away swiftly, before he had a chance to notice that she was trembling.

'I said tell me about yourself,' she said quickly. 'Your name's O'Neill. That's an important Irish name, isn't it?'

'It is,' he said, soberly.

'Do you have an illustrious family history?'

'Most certainly. My great-grandfather was a blind harper of unrivalled skill, the last of the wandering bards. One of my really famous ancestors was known as Shane the Proud — as bloodthirsty and merciless a fellow as you could hope to meet. He supported Mary Queen of Scots against Elizabeth. Poor Shane lost his family fortune to a bastard half-brother, Matthew, who was a friend of Queen Elizabeth's. She withdrew her support for Shane, and recognised Matthew's son Brian as the Earl of Tyrone. Shane burned down Armagh for that. He got murdered eventually. His head was spiked up on Dublin Castle.'

'Now I know where you get your temper,' Rosanna laughed. Finbar took that as a compliment.

'But you!' she said. 'What about yourself? The truth, now. I'd really like to know.'

There was a pause while he sipped his drink. 'Not a lot to tell. I'm twenty years old, no strings, no ties, no family. No one cares for me, and I care for no one, and that's the way I like it. I'm a professional drifter.'

He told her his family hailed from Ballyferriter, where his relatives made their living growing parsley to sell to the French. He'd done everything from factory work to journalism, and, as she knew already, was quite a scholar in his own right; he knew the Middle East well, and had rubbed shoulders with archaeologists and eminent men — including Rosanna's beloved Edison, whom he considered to be no great loss.

'But you always seem so bitter,' Rosanna probed. 'Why? You must have been badly hurt by something. Or somebody, I suppose. '

Finbar laughed harshly. 'Perceptive little thing, aren't you? An amateur psychologist. What do you want — the real sordid story of my life?'

'Why not?' She wanted to touch him. She wanted to heal his hurt. He looked so angry, so enclosed, that she thought at first she had gone too far. But then, suddenly, he began to talk and she knew she had been right.

The story that unfolded made Rosanna's heart ache for him. He had wandered off to Greece, young and starry-eyed, and there fallen hard for a local girl. Against all advice he had married her, too young, too foreign, too naïve. Within months the marriage had foundered. He couldn't take the responsibility, or the smothering embrace of her family which alternated with flashes of hostility when his foreignness showed itself. He had already decided to get out of it when they discovered she was pregnant, so he stayed — but she died having his child, and the child died also. He swore never to get mixed up with women again on a permanent basis. As he was attractive (he didn't suffer from modesty) he managed well enough.

So now he drifted around the Middle East, picking up any work that was going, and doing courier work for tour companies when he was really pushed.

Finbar subsided into morose silence. Rosanna wished him good night, sorry that she had not really been able to lighten his spirits. When he realised that she was going, he pulled himself together and took her hand again.

'Running away, Rosie?'

She faced him squarely.

'I don't need to run from you, O'Neill,' she said. 'You're running so fast from yourself.'

He let go of her hand as if she had slapped him.

'Well, if I am, that's my business.'

'Quite.'

Back in her room, Rosanna took the Horus statue out of her handbag and placed him upright on the bedside table. His supercilious little face took in the basic facilities, and frowned. He was obviously used to better things. Rosanna flung herself down on top of the bedcover, and after a while, she slept.

Chapter Twelve

The next day Abu Samil took charge. They left just after dawn to visit Tel-el-Amarna, the special holy city of Tutankhamun's supposed father, Pharaoh Ikhnaton. In a roofed cart hauled by a belligerent yellow tractor, they were trundled towards the mud-brick palace of the so-called 'heretic king'. All that remained of it was a jumbled heap of ruined walls.

Rosanna picked up a small brick that must have been formed at the time of the prophet Moses, a brick that might have been patted together by the hands of a tormented Hebrew captive, bitter from Pharaoh's refusal to let them go, reeling under the newly-imposed order that they had to chop their own straw to add to the clay. As she turned her brick, it brought a lump to her throat to see chopped pieces of straw still obvious in the mix. She tenderly wrapped the brick in a piece of stockinette bandage.

'What on earth are you doing?' Finbar's sudden intrusion made Rosanna jump, as usual. He had been watching her.

'Just bagging a souvenir,' she said.

'A lump of Nile mud? Are you crazy?'

'Mind your own business!'

'If you're going to fill your suitcase with lumps of mud, you needn't bother asking me to carry it for you!' His face wore its most irritating, superior smirk.

'I wouldn't dream of asking you for anything,' she said icily.

'It'll crumble anyway,' he scoffed. Rosanna carried off her treasure to a safer distance. She wouldn't have put it past Finbar to snatch it off her and crumble it up there and then, just for the pleasure of tormenting her.

After half an hour they were called back to the wagon, and prepared for their chug across a stretch of flat, empty desert to the foot of distant cliffs. It was a melancholy site, the royal necropolis. Ikhnaton, apparently, had strong family feelings: he had given orders that if any of his loved ones should die elsewhere in Egypt, they should be brought back here for burial, and all his close relatives had been interred at this site, except two — his wife and Tutankhamun.

The gang prepared their cameras, the guide displayed his gold teeth, and Finbar abandoned them all and shinned up the rocky backdrop to a vantage point where he could enjoy the breeze and be alone. They were all eager to enter the tunnels and chambers; only Rosanna seemed aware that they were not just sightseeing but about to go poking about in the privacy of family graves.

She hung back, trying to convince herself that she was being over-squeamish. The tragedies, after all, were so ancient. There was an abandoned loneliness about these tombs — no more grieving relatives; even most tourists avoided them. There were no exciting mortuary temple ruins on show; just a series of gloomy and unprepossessing openings in the rocks.

The group soon disappeared from view, but Rosanna decided she would rather talk to Finbar. Gingerly, she began to clamber up the rocks to where he perched in splendid isolation, gazing out at the pattern of tracks that crisscrossed the desert plain below.

He must have known she was coming, but he didn't turn his head. He just sat there, as still as a statue, until she was virtually upon him.

'Mind if I join you?'

He turned then, his face wearing a faraway look, which was replaced by irritation.

'What's up with you? I thought you'd be busily burrowing away by now. Or perhaps you think you might find a nice piece of rock up here for a souvenir. Help yourself.'

'Don't be silly. I only wanted to talk.'

'But I, my dear, wanted to be alone — as you might have guessed if you'd any sensitivity in that pretty head of yours.'

'Oh.' The snub hurt like a physical blow. 'I'm sorry. I didn't —'

'No, no! Come and sit down. I didn't mean to snap at you. Look, I'm sorry. Truly.' Finbar fumbled in his pocket for his cigarettes and offered her one. 'Here — will this do for an apology?'

'No. Not really,' Rosanna said. He put one in his own mouth and lit it, cupping his hand around the flame against the breeze.

'I guess I always bite your head off,' he said gravely.

'Yes. You do. I wonder why you always do that?'

'You have that effect on me. I get nervous in your company.'

'It's just as well we'll only be in each other's company for a few more days, then,' Rosanna said tartly. 'Imagine what fun we'd have if we were together forever.'

Finbar raised an eyebrow. 'There's no point in proposing to me,' he said with a wicked grin. 'I'm not the marrying kind.'

'I realise that!' she laughed. 'In any case, only an idiot would ever consider marrying you.'

A shudder of pain flashed through his eyes. Rosanna could have bitten her tongue off.

'Quite,' he said. He stood up and brushed off his denims.

'Oh, Finbar, I'm terribly sorry! You made me angry, that's all. I just blurted that out. You know I didn't mean anything.'

'Forget it,' he said curtly. 'I shouldn't have opened my big mouth to you yesterday. My past life is none of your concern.'

'Why do we always have this effect on each other?' Rosanna wailed.

Finbar looked at her oddly.

'You make me remember things I would rather forget,' he said. 'And I *do* want to be alone. OK?'

'It's a free world.'

'Hmm,' he said. 'Is it, I wonder? Just leave me alone to get over this mood, eh? I promise I'll make a fuss of you later.'

'There's no need.'

'Well, we'll see.' He made a fist and buffeted her very gently on the jaw. Rosanna sighed as she watched him climb further up the rocks. She supposed she ought to make the effort to go down and inspect the Amarna tombs. They had very special wall-paintings. It really did seem silly to come all that way and then miss them out.

And yet ... A strange lethargy was possessing her, as if something was physically trying to prevent her from moving. She stared out at the blinding sands, the plain sizzling in the heat haze. Her body seemed to be as heavy as lead. She tried to move her arm, but the effort was too much. The breeze fanned the curls on her forehead. She lay back limply against the rock, in a kind of numb paralysis, watching the wind whip up dust devils in the great empty plain below her.

* * *

The palace is set upon a height, reached by a three-terraced garden. Beyond the palace lie the servants' quarters, the kitchens and the bakery, the cellars which hold the huge red wine-jars, and the stables where Menkheperre keeps his great black steeds. Around the estate is a high, forbidding wall.

It is the Heb-sed feast, the festival of the god, who, at the concluding of the mysteries, will be reborn on the horizon. The Pharaoh must go through this simulacrum of death, although he is unwilling and finds it distasteful.

Rameses' health grows worse each month, and he has lost a great deal of weight. It is as though he is being eaten up from within. The last time I saw him, he was like a living corpse, he was so withered, so old.

I found out that he has sent a desperate message to the Hittite king, asking to borrow the statue of the goddess Ishtar, in the hope that it will restore his physical vigour. I doubt the Hittite king will agree to it. In view of the hostilities between our kingdoms, I cannot believe that he will.

He comes into the large reception hall which leads into the biggest living room in the palace, its ceiling supported by eight columns decorated with plants and animals. The narrow stone-barred windows are set very high, in order to temper the harsh daylight.

Rameses II, Living Horus. He looks in a desperate mood. He never enjoys putting on the Shroud of Osiris, to go through the routine of death and rebirth for the priests. You would think it would take more than the ride around the temple in his electrum-plated chariot to convince anyone, let alone himself — or me — that his powers have been rejuvenated and he has been born again, Horus on the horizon.

He sent generous presents to the Hittite — gold, lapis lazuli, weapons, chariots, even a consignment of beautiful young girls. He was wasting his time. The Hittite king has no intention of risking his country's powerful goddess-ka in Egypt. In his opinion, too, Rameses should do his duty, and give his body back to the soil.

I watch him emerging from the Chapel of Shuyet-Re, dedicated to the Queen Nefertari — the palace where the god passes on his special blessings to the royal daughters of pure blood, the receivers of the god, the chosen vessels.

Outside the Chapel the workmen are busy putting the finishing touches to yet another colossus of His Majesty as he used to be — striding, strong, in the full flood of his power. Look — he reaches out and touches the giant stone foot, a foot baked by the power of the sun. The warmth runs up into his fingers.

The statue has more warmth in it than he does. He is shrivelling up while he still lives. The Horus-power is departing, whether he wills it or not. His gift to the soil is long overdue. How can he still cling on? I have nothing but contempt for him.

The priests make him demonstrate at Heb-sed every year now that he is becoming weaker. They watch him like hawks. He could destroy them with a word, but their cold eyes are destroying him. Eating up his vigour, wasting him.

I might be able to pity him if I did not fear him so much.

In the palace the women have let loose their hair and are giving vent to their sadness and despair.

He goes into the one room that I am not allowed to enter. In this room my sister, the youngest and most royal bride of my father, is dying. Everyone knows it, although it is sacrilege to speak of it. Tashery is of the purest of pure blood, the daughter of the Pharaoh and his sister-wife, raised separately until the time that she could become the vessel for her father. She is only twelve years old, but she showed the signs of womanhood early. Our father used her, a year ago, at the last Heb-sed.

Tashery became pregnant, she bore him a child, another daughter, but it died. And now Tashery herself is dying. She was too young, they say. Her body should never have been used for a marriage-vessel so soon — but the Pharaoh was ruthless, desperate to cling to his power, and poor Tashery was old enough to dedicate each month her divine blood.

And now I too am ready, a woman — not of the purest line, but born in the palace. My sacred blood has been seen each month; I am ready to receive the god. I cannot hide it any longer. Word has gone from my servants to the Queen, and from the Queen to the Pharaoh. If Tashery dies ... if Tashery dies ...

* * *

There was a brown hand shaking her shoulder. Rosanna looked up to find the guide hovering over her with a perplexed look on his face.

85

'Come down now, missy,' he said. 'Everyone gone to see the tombs. Special tombs here. Not like elsewhere.' Finding a tourist who did not rush without hesitation into one of his prized burial-places was obviously disturbing him.

'Actually,' Rosanna apologised, 'I'm not feeling very well.' She could not get the tremors of fear and foreboding out of her head. It was more than just vivid imagination; it was sinister. She was beginning to have a great deal of difficulty in disentangling her vivid mental pictures from reality.

The temperature had soared, and sweat ran down Rosanna's back as she trudged back down to the tree-line, where she found Abu Samil in the shade of an old acacia. He could see at once that she was suffering.

'Miss Rose, would you care for some tea?'

'You don't really mean it, do you?'

'Of course. Come and sit down. I will show you how one survives in these terrible conditions.'

Rosanna smiled gratefully and sat beside him. In no time he had lit a fire from dead thorn twigs, produced from his knapsack all the essentials of tea-making — down to a small black kettle and several glasses — and set the kettle, filled with a mixture of water, tea-leaves and sugar, to boil.

'You must be more careful to work out what you can and what you cannot do,' he said. 'Take no risks, my dear. You have a fair skin. If you begin to feel exhausted, stay in the shade.'

'I won't keep apologising,' she said ruefully. 'It gets to be a bore. What do you think the temperature is?'

'Too hot for you,' Abu Samil smiled.

'But I don't want to miss anything!'

'Ah — if only we could do all that we want to in life! But it cannot be so. To achieve all that one's heart desires must surely take many lifetimes.'

The Professor and Finbar appeared. Trust them to smell out the tea, Rosanna thought grudgingly. Finbar sat down next to her in one lithe movement, quite at home in this wilderness of searing heat.

Abu Samil picked up the kettle and, with a flourish, poured tea into one of the glasses. While Rosanna sipped the scalding brew, Abu Samil presided over his simple arrangements like a king.

'More?'

'Thank you, but I'm sure Finbar would appreciate the next glass.'

'Finbar will wait until you have had sufficient, my dear.'

Rosanna dared not look at Finbar's face to see how he enjoyed being put down. It was selfish, but the temptation to annoy him was too great. She smiled sweetly at Abu Samil and held out her glass.

'In that case — perhaps just a little, if you can spare it?'

Finbar stretched himself out lazily on the sand and tipped his hat forward over his face. Underneath the battered khaki Rosanna was sure he was smiling his contemptuous smile. His shirt was unbuttoned. She fought off a fierce longing to pour the boiling tea straight onto his navel.

'Thank you, my friend.' She handed her glass back to the guide. 'That helped me more than you realise.'

She stood up. Finbar lifted his hat and squinted at her.

'Now where do you think you're going?' he demanded.

'Just for a look around. Please don't concern yourself on my behalf.'

He sighed and stood up. 'I have never known a young woman to be such a nuisance as you, Miss March,' he said. But he did not say it unpleasantly, so Rosanna smiled at him. He led her away from their little campfire. Above them, the others were making their way down to the acacia.

Suddenly Finbar's gaze shifted, and he flung himself at Rosanna with a cry. She hit the ground with a thump, and lay there winded. When she tried to struggle up, Finbar held her back with one arm.

'Look!' He crouched on his heels and pointed to a mark in the sand, just where she had been about to tread. His sharp eyes had seen what she would never have noticed —

the telltale series of S-shaped furrows made by a horned viper. The snake was almost completely buried, waiting in ambush for some careless rodent or unwary explorer. Only a small part of its head was visible.

'Abu Samil!' Finbar called, still holding Rosanna back. Her face had gone white. The guide heard the sharp tone of his voice, and when he appeared he took in the situation immediately.

'Snake?'

'Viper.'

'I come, do not fear!' He rushed forward with his stick, with its small fork at the end, and pinned the viper to the ground by the back of its neck. The snake writhed furiously, coiling its body into the air, and opening enormous jaws to hiss at them.

'Shall I kill it?' Abu Samil asked. The question was never answered, for suddenly there was a loud report and the snake's head was spattered all over the sand. Rosanna spun round to see Professor Bloxham standing a few feet away, holding a gun.

They all stared from the snake to the gun. The Professor blew on the barrel like a cowboy, and put the gun back under his shirt. Abu Samil and Finbar straightened up and stared at him.

'Where did you get that gun?' It was Finbar who spoke first. The others, hearing the commotion, came running from all directions. The Professor picked up the snake by its tail.

'Where did you get that gun?' Finbar repeated.

'One travels prepared,' the Professor shrugged. Blood from the snake dripped onto his shoe. 'Anyone handy at curing snakeskins?' No one spoke. 'Seems a pity.' He tossed the snake away.

Finbar bent to help Rosanna to her feet. She had been near the snake when the gun was fired. To her annoyance, she found she was trembling. Finbar put an arm round her.

'You all right?' he asked with a worried frown. She nodded. 'I suppose I owe you an apology for knocking you over,' he said gruffly.

'I suppose I owe you thanks for saving my life,' she replied.

'No need to exaggerate. I doubt if the viper would have made a move unless you had actually trodden on it. They're scared stiff of humans.'

'With good reason, apparently,' she said, staring at the Professor's back as he sauntered off. Finbar handed her over to Mike and the girls, and strode in pursuit of him.

'Poor old Monty,' said Mike. 'Looks like he's in for a spanking.'

Rosanna was not sorry for him.

'Did you know he carried a gun?' she asked.

Mike shook his head. 'Who would have guessed it? That puts our dear old Prof in rather a different light, doesn't it? Well, well, well.'

'Why shouldn't he carry a gun?' snapped Bertice. 'Seems to me it's a very sensible thing to do out here. We'd probably be a lot safer if we all had guns!'

'How did he get it through Customs?' Joey wondered.

'Don't ask me! Maybe he picked it up here. Maybe his friends —'

'Oh, come on!' Mike was impatient. 'Who the hell cares? If he's breaking the law, that's O'Neill's problem now. Come on, Rosie, cheer up! It was only a snake.'

Chapter Thirteen

A knock at the door made Rosanna sit up drowsily and look
at her watch: 11.30 p.m. The girls had not returned.

Another knock, still gentle, but now insistent. She opened
the door a crack and saw Finbar. He had been smoking a
cheroot, and the scent of it wafted past him into the room.

'Yes?'

'Can I come in?' Without waiting for a reply, he slipped
into the room and closed the door.

'Actually, I've gone to bed,' Rosanna said, crossly. 'I'm
not feeling too well. So if you don't mind —'

'Dodgy tummy? I can give you something for that.'

'No — it's my head and throat. My throat's really sore. I
guess I still can't get used to the hot dry air.'

Finbar nodded. 'Probably. Didn't you bring any aspirin?'

Rosanna could hardly believe her ears. Was that a note
of concern in his voice?

'Well, I did, but I've nearly used it all up.'

Suddenly, glancing past her, he saw the statue of Horus.
He looked as if he had seen a ghost.

'Where the hell did you get that?' he demanded fiercely.
'Who gave it to you?'

'What do you mean?' She frowned, worried by the mixture of anger and fear in his expression.

'Come on, Rosie, you've got to tell me where you got this
from!'

'Why? What business is it of yours?'

'Damn it, will you just accept that it *is* my business. Very much so. Don't you know what that statue is?'

'Of course I do. It's Horus the hawk.'

Finbar picked it up and turned it over thoughtfully.

'Listen, Rosie. I don't know what you know, or what you're hiding from me — but that little statue didn't just come from a tourist shop. Did you have that with you when you came to Egypt?'

'Well, no. I —' Rosanna hesitated, guiltily. His eyes narrowed. She decided she would have to trust him. 'It happened while we were in Cairo. Someone got into my room, and just left it in my luggage.'

'An Egyptian?'

'Yes.'

'You saw him?'

She told him exactly what had taken place. Finbar listened in silence, his face grim.

'Why didn't you tell me before?'

'Well, I — I didn't think it was any —'

'Of my business.' He laughed harshly. 'Let me tell you, young lady, that I am responsible for your safety on this trip, and —'

'My *safety*?' Now she was really alarmed. 'Look, Finbar, I admit I was worried in Cairo, but surely now that we're well away — ?'

'Give me that thing,' he said sternly. She allowed him to button it into the pocket of his shirt. 'You really don't know anything about this, do you?'

Rosanna shook her head, disturbed by his tone and the seriousness with which he had taken the incident.

'I should have told you,' she whispered. 'I'm sorry I didn't.'

'Quite. Let's hope there's no real harm done. I'll keep this. If anything else happens, you're to let me know immediately.'

The old arrogance. He went to the door. Rosanna jumped up after him.

'Finbar! If I'm involved in something, don't you think

you should tell me? What else do you think might happen?'

To Rosanna's amazement, Finbar cupped her face in his hand and kissed her on the nose.

'No, Rosie. I think it best that you don't know anything else. It's safer that way. Does anyone else know about this statue?'

'Mike and Joey. I told them.'

'Don't tell anyone else. Understand?'

'But —'

'Will you trust me?' He was gazing into her eyes. 'Please?'

'All right.'

The Springer girls appeared on the corridor, in high spirits. Finbar nodded to them and wished them all good night.

'Hey!' said Bertice, breezing in. 'What was all that about? We thought you were safely tucked up in bed, not carrying on with Hitler.'

'I was *not* carrying on,' Rosanna lied, blushing. 'And he's not so bad when you get to know him.'

'Oh yes?'

* * *

'Good grief!' The Professor's usually urbane voice had taken on the timbre of real surprise. His exclamation was not aimed at anyone in particular, but was voiced for the benefit of the entire bus. 'There's been a very nasty earthquake in Bulgaria,' he informed them, peering over the top of the paper. 'Thousands feared dead. Landslides. Avalanches of mud. Villages cut off, fear of disease, and so on. My God, I was only there ...'

The Professor had managed to acquire a newspaper printed in English. It was three days old, but full of reminders about the world they had left behind. Not everyone wished to be reminded, but the Professor was not the sort of man who could sit and read the news in silence.

The earthquake had apparently been quite catastrophic. Rosanna found herself drawing a mental map to visualise how far away Bulgaria was. She did not fancy being stuck down an ancient tomb-tunnel if any follow-up tremors should reach as far as the Nile.

Fortunately their new destination — the Temple of Abydos, built by the megalomaniac Rameses II — was above ground. They expected to be impressed; it would be their first temple, and it had once been the most sacred shrine in the world.

Rosanna glanced shyly at Finbar as he handed round their entrance tickets. He gave her a conspiratorial wink that set her heart fluttering.

'And how's my girl this morning?' he said. He was smiling at her, a genuine open smile that bore no cynicism.

'Fine. Just fine,' she said. She was lying — her throat hurt like mad — but there was nothing the matter with the vibes that were zinging through her bloodstream.

'The burial-place of Osiris,' he said. 'Excited?'

'Brimming over.' Their hands were nearly touching as they began to walk together towards the entrance. 'But Isis buried Osiris in parts,' Rosanna said. 'What part was buried here?'

'His head,' said Finbar. 'That's why Abydos is such an important shrine.'

'It seems so strange to think of a dead god. It's a contradiction in terms, isn't it? How can a god die?'

'He didn't, of course. He had passed on the seed. You see, Osiris and Horus are really one: the vital force, the force of the sun. And the Osiris-Horus never dies. Neither,' he added softly, 'does the soul that loves him. He is the cause and means of resurrection, the god-man who suffers, dies and rises again, and through him shall all who believe in him be made alive.'

They wandered through Rameses' great courtyard, between the rows of massive columns covered with hieroglyphs. Rosanna looked sideways at Finbar. 'Isn't that what the Christians teach of Christ?'

'Of course.' Finbar smiled again. 'The younger brothers, who came so late to the faith. They love their Osiris-Horus, as we love ours. But they forget that we loved him untold centuries before they came to recognise him in Jesus.'

Rosanna noticed that he had said 'we', identifying himself with the Egyptians, but she let that pass. They moved into the sanctuary, with its seven dark shrines.

'But Jesus wasn't just a myth; he was an actual historical person who lived and walked on earth,' she said.

'As Horus does, again and again,' Finbar replied. Rosanna raised an eyebrow. 'Yes, Rosanna, no need to be sceptical. What use is a god to mankind if he's so far away that no one can ever know him? We *need* our gods to live and breathe, and walk among us. In the days of the pharaohs, the god entered the chief queen in order to bestow the sacred seed — and so her son was always the son of the god. When he became pharaoh, he was recognised as Living Horus. At his death he became Osiris, and his human remains were buried for the fertility and benefit of the land. The new Horus took his place.'

She wanted to say it was not always the chief queen ...

Neither of them had heard the Professor's approach.

'For heaven's sake,' he broke in, 'Rosie is far too young to be burdened with all this theology!'

Rosanna winced. Finbar must have been annoyed at the intrusion too, for he patted her gently on the arm, then turned abruptly and walked off. Rosanna was furious. Without his company the famous ruins suddenly lost all their interest and became just a pile of old stones.

She stormed back to the Hall of the Columns, where she sat on the small rim around one of the bases and cast a wary eye over the enormous bats that flickered out of the masonry. The Professor and Abu Samil joined her.

'You look upset, my dear,' Abu Samil said smoothly.

'I am upset,' said Rosanna sharply. 'I'm beginning to think Egypt is too much for me.'

'Don't be so serious,' Abu Samil smiled. 'This is a

strange and magic place, Miss Rose. Strange things can happen, here in Egypt; but they are not real, you know.'

'What do you mean?'

'Here, where so many centuries lie undisturbed, what is our brief moment? It is no part of real time. A lifetime can pass in a flash, or a mere moment be extended into eternity. It is time-out-of-time, and you make it what you will.'

'Perhaps.' She knew what he meant, and in her heart she felt he was right, but she was impatient with him. It was Finbar she wanted to talk to, and they had driven him away.

'Is this what is troubling you?' asked Abu Samil. 'Time and memory are strange things. We forget what we did yesterday, but if we close our eyes to this noisy world, we find that we can sometimes see glimpses that reach far beyond our usual horizons.'

'Do you think so?' Rosanna asked. 'Do you think we could have previous lives — and vague memories of what we've done before?'

'It's possible, isn't it?' the Professor nodded. 'But there again, who can really say? Reincarnation is fashionable now, hadn't you noticed?'

'Yes, I had. But until I came to Egypt I don't believe I ever had a flicker of anything like that. But here, my imagination's running riot. I keep getting odd glimpses —'

'Imagination?' Abu Samil let his words slide gently. 'I would like to hear what you have experienced — but only if you wish to tell us.'

'I think my body is having a real struggle to adjust,' Rosanna said quietly, 'and when I'm at my most exhausted, my mind takes over and concocts things.'

'Dreams?'

'Yes — but more than dreams. Sometimes I'm wide awake, or at least I think I am. I had an experience like that at Tel-el-Amarna — a whole long, connected sequence, that must have actually gone through my mind in one quick flash. The strange thing is that they all seem to be about a particular person — a young man.' She blushed.

'With whom you are perhaps in love?' prompted Abu Samil.

'Yes. And there's another man in the dreams, a man who hates him. A pharaoh. And maybe he hates me as well — I'm not sure.'

'Do you always figure in these dreams?'

'Oh yes. Always. Except it's not really me. I'm much younger, about thirteen.'

'And very much in love.' The Professor laughed aloud. 'Wishful thinking?'

Rosanna despised him. 'Ah, well,' she said, wishing she had never opened her mouth. She stood up. 'You're right. That's probably it.'

She walked away to the stalls outside the temple and poked about amongst the scarabs, necklaces and postcards. There was, of all things, a row of green tartan penknives hanging from a wire at the back. Rosanna got the man to unfasten one of them and hand it over.

'No sign of Horus, I see,' she said, as Finbar joined her.

'Why don't you buy one of these?' he asked, picking up a corroded bronze statuette of Bastet the Cat. It was supposed to be a genuine antique, and it certainly looked very old — but Finbar told Rosanna the modern villagers made them, and the green patina had been created by a ducking in some very modern acid. A few sentences in Arabic to the vendor, and Finbar passed over a handful of money, dumped the cat and the penknife into Rosanna's hands, and set off in the direction of the bus.

'What's up with him?' Mike asked, joining her. 'I see his attitude to you hasn't improved, and yet here he is showering you with presents!'

'Hardly showering.'

'What did you do to earn those?'

'Don't be ridiculous. He knows I'll pay him back. Let's face it, I would probably have been conned out of a fortune.'

Chapter Fourteen

They had another temple to visit that day: Dendera, the beautiful Temple of Hathor, goddess of love, once patronised by her famous devotee Cleopatra.

'We can stay here until nightfall,' Finbar announced. 'We'll push on as soon as it's dark, but it's worth hanging on for a glimpse of Dendera when the floodlights are switched on.'

They piled out onto soft sand that lapped their ankles. Yellow and black dogs lay panting in the sun, and twitched their ears at the unexpected disturbance. There was an air of languid indolence that began in the palm trees where the green bee-eaters hung swaying in the fronds, and spread out over the ancient House of Joy.

They passed some unprepossessing ruins which had been birth-houses, places specially set apart for the ritual unions, when the queens received the god and incarnated a new Horus. Immediately in front of them was a great courtyard, now buried in loose sand, and a huge wall topped by a row of sacred cobras and square columns bearing the face of Hathor on all sides, so that the Mother could simultaneously watch over all four directions of the earth.

Rosanna felt her pulse quicken. She ought to have been moved by Abydos, but it had left her cold. Here, for some reason, there was a singing in her veins, an anticipation of joy and satisfaction.

'Miss Rose!' She looked round, still in a daze, at Abu Samil.

'Miss Rose, my dear — you forgot your ticket. Here it is.'

'Thank you,' she murmured, and turned back to the great wall that loomed before her, gazing up at the face of Hathor. The full, luscious lips were curved in a smile; the swathes of heavy curls clustered on her shoulders. It was the round, enticing face of a beauty queen, quivering with invitation and expectation. The eyes were wide and seductive, but they were also shrewd; they took in everything. As the mortals approached, the eyes fixed them, examined them with a mild curiosity, then drew them into the universal embrace.

'Come to me, my little ones,' the stones whispered. 'Forget your cares, forget your pains. Let me wipe away all tears from your eyes. There shall be no more pain.'

Abu Samil followed Rosanna's gaze. 'Why do you hesitate?' he asked softly.

She looked at the corniche of sacred cobras and drew in her breath. They were not stone. They were living things, alert, watching.

'What do you feel, Miss Rose? Do you feel the presence here?'

'I feel —' She paused. A tingling had started in her hands. The cobras were shifting nervously, their heads raised to strike, their forked tongues poised and ready to spit fire. 'I feel confused.'

'Fear?'

'Why should I fear?' He had caught her uneasy glance. 'And yet — there is something. A danger.' She shook her head. A row of sculptured snakes, worn smooth by centuries of sand and wind, were all that guarded this temple now. 'I'm being silly,' she said. 'Let's go inside.'

On the threshold Abu Samil bowed.

'Why did you do that?' Rosanna whispered. 'It's only a ruin.'

'The House of the Mother?' he chided. 'The House of Joy? Come, Miss Rose, you are holding back. Tell me what you really see.'

She peered into the shadows of the lofty columns that crowded the hall. They were feminine, opulent, with intricately-carved capitals.

'A memory,' she said, 'of something that was wonderful once.' She was puzzled. She wanted to sit in the dark and let the atmosphere take her.

'Give me your hand,' Abu Samil said softly. 'Now close your eyes.'

Rosanna did as he instructed her. He led her to one of the columns and placed her hands upon it. A kind of shock made her heart lurch painfully. He covered her hands with his own, refusing to let her draw hers away. As he felt her tremor, a satisfied smile lit up his features. 'This time, my dear, you must open your eyes. It is time. Tell me again what you can see. What you really see.'

'I can see —' Rosanna looked around, shaken by what she saw. She was no longer in a world of long-dead rock and sand; she was a midget, a tiny mortal, intruding in a huge magic forest of papyrus-stems growing to the scale of the gods.

'Green,' she whispered. 'It's all green!'

'Go on.'

Words would not come. She moved from pillar to pillar, touching them, stroking them, pausing to trace a finger over a hieroglyph.

'Yes, my dear one, I know that you see it. Look. Here — here! You are in a vast papyrus thicket.' She nodded. 'The floor is the Nile, the water of life. Its sap feeds the papyrus clumps springing from the silt, swarming with birds and reptiles. You see the pillars, flowers of lotus in bud or in full blossom. Their bases are entwined with leaves. Overhead the sky is heavy with stars.'

'I see it all,' she whispered.

Abu Samil led her into the sanctuary, where she gazed at a representation of a pharaoh burning incense before the two gods Horus and Hathor.

'And our Lady?' he murmured. 'How do you see her?'

Rosanna's face was aglow.

'What of Hathor the Beautiful — she who first suckled the infant Horus in the hidden places of the Delta; she who loved him more than life itself, and became his beloved here at Dendera? Do you see the innocent Maid, whose love Horus won? Or she who was Mother, and cherished the infant and fed him from her own breast? Or she who watched over his death and still loved? Who do you see, when you bow before the Great Mother, the lover of the god?'

The great grasses were swaying, the papyrus hissed, the river lapped green about her ankles.

He would rise like the sun at the dawning of the world, emerging from the blue lotus-flower, to dominate the waters of primeval chaos. He would rise, he would come. The blue lotus-bud unfurling, opening. The sun, the golden-silver sun bursting through the reeds.

'Give me your answer, Miss Rose,' Abu Samil's voice insisted. 'Tell me — who do you see?'

'I see the lover,' she whispered. 'The lover.'

She did not see Finbar come up behind her. He slid his arms around her waist. It did not seem strange.

She felt the god at her side. They were together in the misty green air, folded in love in a garden of lotus blossoms. No words. Stillness. The flapping wings of the night heron, the bright-eyed timid fox creeping from the desert to the water. The slow, soft fall of the heavy night dew. She trembled in his arms. Desire burnt through her. Light. Fire.

Rosanna shuddered to reality. Abu Samil was watching them, his black eyes smouldering. He was angry. 'You have intruded on us, Finbar,' he said. 'Leave Miss Rose alone.'

'What business is it of yours?'

'I am aware of her growing friendship with Mike Cooper, even if you cannot see it!'

Rosanna shook them both off. The green light faded. Flowers and fronds slipped silently within the stone. It was dark in the sanctuary; night had fallen. Outside the floodlights were being switched on, and a huge moon was rising. The green oasis petrified, and hid its secrets from the secular world.

* * *

Everyone was aware that the driver, too, was tired. It was a heart-stopping lunatic dash down the highway which, mercifully, had been plunged into a concealing darkness so that they could not see the crashed vehicles. At around eight o'clock they arrived in Luxor.

Civilisation. Bright lights. Glamorous hotels with famous names; romantic palm-tree walks along the river bank where glittering tourist cruisers were moored, and where families took the night air or relaxed at inviting little bistros. Floodlit, exotic piles of ruins. Chemists' shops!

And across the Nile, in the west, the sad watch-fires winking in the Land of the Dead.

Even in their haggard state, the explorers' eyes lit up as the bus coated with desert dust chugged up the main thoroughfare of Luxor and pulled up at the Panorama. The garden gate opened a chink. There was a flood of Arabic; then the gate was pulled wide and Finbar was seized in the embrace of a young man who seemed genuinely delighted to see him.

'This is Muhammad,' Finbar announced when he had been released. 'He doesn't speak much English, but if you go slowly he'll probably work out what you want. We're late. Your rooms are all ready, and dinner has been waiting for the last two hours!'

They shuffled wearily in and dumped their cases in the courtyard while Finbar sorted out the keys. Behind a pretty trellis they could see two long trestles set out for dinner in the open air. Suddenly everyone was very hungry.

'I've had a word with Muhammad,' said Finbar in

Rosanna's ear. 'You get a room to yourself. OK?'

'Thanks. Do I have to pay any extra?'

'We'll argue about that later. Just behave yourself, will you?'

'And what is that supposed to mean?'

'We'll argue about that later, too, Now, get moving. We need to eat, and put back some fluids.'

Dinner was a splendid meal, but Rosanna's throat — which had been steadily getting worse — stung so violently when she swallowed that she left early again, and took her very last aspirin.

Even with the fan on it was too hot to sleep, and Rosanna was quite gratified when Mike and Joey turned up later to see how she was.

'We were hoping you weren't flat out,' Mike said.

'What's up?'

'Abu Samil's fixed up a trip into town, and we want you with us.'

'Oh, Mike — I don't know. I'm not feeling too good ...'

'What's the matter, Rosie?' Joey cried. 'You're missing all the fun.'

'I'm talking about you and me, and the moonlight ...' Mike smiled. Rosanna gave him a long, cool look. 'No, seriously, Monty and Abu Samil have been concocting something between them, and it involves you.'

'What do you mean?'

'There's an old perfume-seller here who can hypnotise people, and track down their past lives,' Joey said. 'The Prof said you were into all that, so he wants you to volunteer to be the guinea pig.'

'Did he send you up to get me?'

Mike grinned. 'He reckoned I had more charm.'

Rosanna laughed, but she wriggled away when he tried to slip his arms round her.

'I think my charm's fading,' he muttered ruefully. 'What's happened, Rosie? I thought you and me were beginning to get something going, but now you've gone all cold on me. Is it something I've done? Or not done?'

'No, of course not,' she said quickly. 'Nothing like that.'

'Is it O'Neill?' Rosanna felt Mike's grip tighten, and she turned her head, not wanting to meet his eyes. 'It *is* O'Neill!' he cried. 'Don't fool with him, Rosie. You'll only get hurt.'

'There's nothing between him and me,' she said, flushing.

'Come out with us tonight, then,' he said, holding her at arm's length. 'It'll be good for a laugh.'

'You never come out with us,' added Joey. 'Come on, Rosie, what do you say?'

'Sounds a bit dangerous to me.'

'Not if Abu Samil knows the man. He'll make sure nothing goes wrong.'

Feeling more than a little apprehensive, she went to gather up her things. Then there was another knock on the door. Rosanna froze.

'That's probably Monty,' Mike said cheerfully, pulling it open. It wasn't. It was Finbar. He didn't see Joey, and it took him two seconds to come to the wrong conclusion.

'What do you want?' Mike asked coldly. Finbar gave him one of his most contemptuous smiles.

'I was just looking in to see if Rosanna was all right,' he said. 'Apparently my fears for her health were all in vain. Good night.'

Before Rosanna could even open her mouth he was off down the corridor, leaving her wretched and embarrassed. Mike was delighted.

When they joined the Professor in the foyer, Finbar was back with his Egyptian friends, ignoring them. A *calesh* had been ordered, one of the horse-drawn carriages that were the main form of transport in Luxor. Just before they drove off, Muhammad came over with a package for Rosanna.

'Mister Finbar say to give you these,' he said.

It was aspirin tablets. She looked up to thank Finbar, but he had his back turned and refused to look round.

Chapter Fifteen

Abu Samil met them at the carriage-stand outside the Winter Palace Hotel. He was not alone. With him was a young man whom he introduced as his brother Saud.

Saud was a member of the Luxor tourist police, and proud of it. Instead of a djellaba, he wore his smart white shirt and trousers, with the armband of his rank. He was much younger than Abu Samil, with a shock of long black hair and thick lustrous eyelashes of such length that Rosanna thought he was wasted in his profession. He ought to have been a film star.

'We didn't know you had a brother here, Abu Samil.'

The guide laughed. 'An Egyptian has brothers everywhere,' he said.

Luxor, for all its tourist trade, was still only a small town, and once off the main road that ran along by the Nile, it was hardly touched by the western world. They went through the backstreets to an alleyway that served as an extension to a small bazaar.

'This is the place,' said Abu Samil. He stopped before the doorway of the perfume-seller's cubicle. On a high divan behind a trestle table sat an ancient man with a toothy grin, heavy eyebrows and an enormous jaw. He looked slightly dazed, as if the reek from his own essences had intoxicated him. 'And this is my uncle Youssef.'

The old man kissed the two brothers, then raised his thin arm and beckoned them all to come in and sit down.

104

Rosanna was pushed to the front. They squeezed into his room and sat below him, on lesser divans.

'You are welcome,' he told them gravely. 'Most welcome, friends of my nephew.'

He fixed Rosanna with a piercing stare which increased in intensity as Abu Samil explained why they had come.

'Madam is willing?' Youssef asked. Her timid nod was taken as assent. He smiled.

'An English girl,' he said softly, partly to his nephew, partly to himself. 'This is the first time, Abu Samil, that you bring to me an English girl for exploration of the mind.'

'You will find this girl very sympathetic,' said the guide. 'You may proceed with her. But gently.'

'As you wish,' Youssef murmured. His stare had made Rosanna quite uncomfortable. Now his eyes softened a little, and he took her hand. 'Nothing to fear,' he said softly. 'Everything to learn. Be at ease, my dear young lady, and give me your confidence.'

It was too late to back out. Rosanna uncrossed her legs and sat back on the divan.

The old man picked up a silver pen and held it in front of her.

'Watch the pen,' he said, 'and let your mind be at rest.'

She did as she was told. Slowly Youssef moved the pen back and forth, back and forth, and all the time his eyes burnt into hers. Back and forth, back and forth, until she no longer saw the room, or the pen, or the eyes. He passed his hand in front of her face. There was no reaction.

'Can you hear me, my dear?'

There was a long silence, in which only the breathing of the expectant observers could be heard. The Professor coughed. Rosanna sat like a statue, without blinking, without moving. They scanned her face anxiously.

'She's right off,' muttered Mike. 'Are you sure this sort of thing is safe?'

'Shh! Look!'

Rosanna's lips were moving, but there was no sound. Her breathing seemed heavier.

'Can you hear me?' Youssef asked.

'Yes.' The answer was barely audible, no more than a whisper. 'I hear you.'

The old man leaned forward eagerly. 'Good. Good, my dear. Don't be afraid.'

'I hear.'

'I want you to go back. Back. Before this lifetime. Do you understand what I mean? Take yourself back, as far back as you can remember. Can you do that?'

She nodded.

'Think of the time when you lived here among us. Here in Egypt. Can you remember that, my dear?'

Again, the slight inclination of the head. Abu Samil and the Professor sat up expectantly.

'Do you know who you are?'

'Yes.'

'Tell us your name.'

Her face took on an expression of haunted anxiety. She seemed frightened to look at them. Yet at the same time Mike was sure that she could no longer actually see them in the room. Wherever she was, it was not here. He wanted to touch her, but Youssef stopped him.

'Is something the matter? What is it, child? Can't you tell us your name?'

There was a long pause; then, very hesitantly, 'I must not speak it. It is forbidden.'

Abu Samil's glittering black eyes met the watery ones of his uncle. He nodded for him to continue.

'Who has forbidden it? No one can take your name away from you, foolish one. Don't be afraid. Tell us your name.'

Rosanna's head lolled forward. It was a full minute before she spoke again. Expressions came and went on her face, as if she was grappling with enormous confusion.

106

When she did speak at last, it was in a loud clear voice that made them all jump.

'Nilufer,' she said.

'Can you tell us who you are?'

She drew herself up straight and proud on the divan.

'I am the daughter of User-Maat-Re, the son of the god.'

The Professor whistled softly. 'That's our friend Rameses II,' he said.

Mike winced. 'My God, Rosie *will* be pleased!'

'Why is your name forbidden? Who ordered such a thing?'

'He did.' A spasm of intense pain twisted her features. She was struggling again. To speak of that which was forbidden was costing her dear.

'You mean your father? The Pharaoh?'

'Yes.'

'Why should he order such a thing?'

'Because I must cease to exist. Because I will never give myself to him.' The words came out as a desperate cry. Her face revealed all — despair, fear, distaste, pain.

'I should think not!' exclaimed Mike. 'The dirty old man. No wonder she detested him.'

'There is no need for crudeness.' Saud threw a contemptuous glance at Mike. 'Such a marriage would not have been uncommon in those times. No pharaoh, or child of a pharaoh, would marry outside the sacred blood. As a matter of fact, it is known that Rameses did marry four of his own daughters.'

'Does he want you to marry him?' Youssef asked gently.

'He tried to force me.' She shuddered. 'But he knows that I can never accept him. Not in that way. I have honoured him as my king and my father ...'

'You love another?'

'Yes.' There was another long pause. Abu Samil jogged his uncle's arm to make him continue.

'Tell us about your lover.'

'My father sent him to kill the river-horses. He thought that he would fail, and die. But he killed them all. He was not even wounded!' She laughed bitterly. 'Now my father will send him away again to battle. He knows Menkheperre will not hide from the fighting. He has the Golden Fly from the Hittite wars. My father promotes him and gives him commissions because he wants him to die. But I will not go to him even then! When Menkheperre dies, I will die. I will never marry my father and bear his ka.'

They noticed that despite her defiant words, her hands shook.

'It would be a great honour for you to become a bride of the Pharaoh. Is your lover a prince? Is he your brother?'

'He was born in the palace.'

'Wouldn't she know?' whispered Mike.

Saud shook his head. 'Rameses had ninety-two sons and a hundred and six daughters,' he said simply.

'And he still had time to chase after little Nilufer! My God!'

'Move her forward,' Abu Samil snapped, turning back to his uncle. 'Find out what happened to her.'

'Nilufer!' Youssef leaned forward, his face shining yellow in the candlelight. 'It is now a year later. Can you tell us what happened? Did you marry your prince? Or were you made to marry your father?'

A terrible pallor spread over her skin and she began to shake violently. Beads of sweat broke out on her lip and forehead.

'What is it? Nilufer! What is it that you cannot face, my child?' Youssef's soft voice whispered. 'Let your heart remember, for it is all long past. It will not harm you now.'

Rosanna groaned. Sweat trickled down her agonised face. Mike instinctively leaned towards her, deeply worried. Abu Samil gripped his arm and restrained him. His fingers dug deep. His eyes never left the girl's face.

'Speak, child,' the old man urged. 'Speak now of all that

is in your heart. Let your eyes see, and your mind be at rest.'

'They say I must not see! Never see the light again! The bricklayers are coming. They will seal me up — seal me — behind the wall! They will leave me — leave me! Merciful Hathor, I will try not to fear. Oh Horus!' The cry left her lips, a wail of desolate sadness. 'Horus Hartomes, Horus the Lancer! Where are you? Where have you gone?'

Abu Samil reached out and took her hand. She gripped him as if she was a drowning woman, her expression pure terror.

'Where are you, Nilufer?' he cried hoarsely. 'What do you see?'

But she slumped back and her eyes glazed over.

'It is black. Black, blackness,' she muttered.

Mike leapt up and pushed Abu Samil out of the way.

'That's enough!' he shouted. 'I don't think this was a very clever idea. What are you trying to do? Finish her off?'

'Just find the truth,' said Abu Samil. His voice was hard. In that moment Mike disliked him immensely.

'Get her out of this!' Joey cried. He felt like kicking Youssef.

'You're overreacting, boys,' said the Professor smoothly. 'Sit down and let the old chap finish. He knows what he's doing.'

'And I've heard enough.' Mike grabbed the perfume-seller's sleeve and shook him. 'Bring her out of this! I mean it!'

'Mr Cooper, my dear young sir — your Professor is right!' Mike was not surprised to find Abu Samil taking sides against him. 'We do not wish any harm to Miss Rose, surely you know that? All hypnotic regressions go through a stage of trauma, because quite obviously, all those who have lived before have died. Death is nothing to fear. It is quite natural.'

Mike pulled Rosanna into his arms. She sagged limply against him.

'My God,' he muttered, 'I think you're all mad. Can't you see the state she's in?'

Youssef looked questioningly at his nephew, as if waiting for permission. Abu Samil glowered at Mike, then finally shrugged and nodded. The old man motioned for Mike to put Rosanna down. She sat back on the divan, ashen, unblinking. Youssef muttered some words and waved his hands in front of her face and over her head. Then she blinked, and began to cry.

'It's all right, Rosie. It's OK. Here, drink this.' Joey passed her his water-bottle. Her breath came in great sobs.

'I blame you for this, Abu Samil! You're a bloody fool!' Mike cried furiously. 'I'm not going to take my eyes off you again, so you can just leave her alone from now on.'

The guide lit a cigarette and fixed it delicately in his little black holder. He did not look the least bit repentant.

Mike put his arm round Rosanna and helped her out into the dark street. Behind them, Abu Samil was watching them, scowling thoughtfully.

Chapter Sixteen

'I don't know if I can take another temple just yet,' Mike grumbled, unwrapping a strip of chewing gum. He crumpled the paper into a ball and tossed it down.

'You can't come to Luxor and pass up the visit to Karnak, idiot. Come on, perk up! We've got a heck of a lot to do today.'

'I'd rather go shopping.'

'What for?'

'Hell, Rosie, just for a root around. You can pick up really good stuff here, Luxor's the place for it. They say the villagers across the river turn up fresh tombs and loot the treasures all the time.'

'No kidding?' Rosanna mimicked him. They had driven to the sprawling complex of Karnak; at the entrance they were met by Abu Samil and Saud. Saud strode forward to greet them, and asked politely about Rosanna's health.

'My dear,' said Abu Samil, taking her hand after his brother relinquished it. 'How are you this morning? Are you quite well? I had no intention of upsetting you in any way. I am abject. Your friend was quite right — I was a fool.'

'Please don't be concerned,' Rosanna replied. 'I admit I was a bit frightened, but I was also very interested.' She grinned, thinking of Finbar: he had been almost apoplectic with rage when they came breezing in at three o'clock in the morning, and exceedingly stiff when they breakfasted a mere two hours later.

'Well — let us change the subject,' smiled Abu Samil.

'Saud is to be your guide here. He knows far more about Karnak than I do.'

'I doubt that, brother,' the younger man said graciously.

Abydos and Dendera had been impressive, but even their magnificence was dwarfed by Karnak. Rosanna, however, was in no condition to admire temples and palaces, on however grand a scale. The first suspicions of an unwelcome nausea began as soon as she came out of the sun and into the Great Hall. She tried hard to occupy her mind with other things, but soon she was unable to deny the awful fact that she was about to be sick.

Desperately she made a dash into the searing light of the Central Court, and sat down wretchedly on the ground at the base of a huge obelisk of red granite.

'Miss Rose! My dear lady!' Saud had seen her run and followed her out. 'Oh, my dear lady — you are ill!' He waved angrily at two or three touts who had gathered like vultures about their helpless prey. He handed Rosanna a handkerchief soaked with water from his own bottle.

'Please don't tell Finbar,' she managed to say. 'I don't want him to know.'

'But why not? Why are you so frightened of him? He is just a man — a bad-tempered one, I admit it. But it is his business to know if you are ill.'

'No, no — I'm not ill. I think it was an attack of claustrophobia.'

'In such a huge temple?'

'The pillars ...' Rosanna paused; seeing their closeness and bulk in her mind's eye sent another tremor through her. 'Yes, it was the pillars. They were so close. I felt as if — as if they could shift, somehow, and I would be crushed. I felt shut in by them.'

'You don't feel at home, then?' Saud asked, a sly grin on his handsome face.

'Certainly not!' Rosanna gave him a puzzled glance. 'Why should I?'

Saud extended his arms. 'Behold the mighty works of your great father,' he smiled.

'There seems to be no escape from Rameses,' she muttered. She didn't find it at all funny.

She looked round: it was all magnificent, all overwhelming. Rameses did nothing in a small way. It was not his nature. His arrogance and power pervaded every stone, every corner.

They got up to join the others, who were emerging, blinking, into the courtyard. Suddenly, as Rosanna glanced back over her shoulder, the sick feeling came back with a vengeance. Oh God, she thought, it wasn't claustrophobia — nor lack of sleep.

With appalling fear and horror, she realised she *knew* where she was. Blood hissed in her ears.

She saw the empty courtyard full of white-robed priests; she heard the urgent chant, the tambour's throb, the sistrum's rattle, and she saw the knife flash as the sun's cruel beam struck it. She heard the priests' hoarse cries, saw the red blood spurt from the youth who lay on the altar of the sun. The sacrificial chant rent the air. Her senses reeled.

Yet it was not quite the same. She gasped aloud, and they turned and saw her there. They began to move towards her — but someone's strong arms reached her first, holding her protectively.

'You're here! You didn't abandon me!' she cried, her body trembling as she felt his hand on her waist, his arm pressing her against him. She yearned to feel his mouth touch hers. She seemed to have been waiting for his touch for centuries. He lifted her and carried her into the shade; she clung to him eagerly, but his hands tugged at her wrists, pulling them from around his neck. She lifted her face to his, searching for his lips, but he did not kiss her. Instead there was the shock of cold water on her brow, and when she opened her eyes, she found a ring of anxious faces peering down at her.

'Are you satisfied now?' a cold voice said. It was Finbar, glowering at her, his expression one of pure anger. 'Now you've really made yourself ill.'

Rosanna tried to speak, but no words came. Instead, tears rolled down her cheeks. She shut her eyes and turned her head away.

They thought that her exhausted frame was shaking with a fever, that her tears welled up because of her sickness. They didn't know the real reason — the burning ache of loss that smouldered inside her, the dreadful pain.

* * *

Although Finbar's comments were pretty caustic, Rosanna had to admit that he couldn't have taken better care of her — short of bundling her off to hospital, which she absolutely refused to allow. He settled her comfortably in the shade, and organised a mixture of Coke, salt and sugar to be brought for her. At one point he even dabbed at her brow tenderly with a large white handkerchief. He was being very kind, and Rosanna appreciated that. He was adamant that she should stay put, and even sleep if she could.

'Don't be silly!' she protested, and got to her feet. Finbar sat there, arms folded, and watched her totter a few paces into the searing sunlight. 'Aren't you coming with me?'

'No.'

'Why not?'

'You'll not get far,' he told her calmly. Rosanna knew he was right, but it annoyed her to have to admit it. She came back and sat down next to him, fuming.

They sat with their arms touching. She was aware of his warmth, of something that might have been concern in his eyes when he happened to look at her.

But her heart was tight and heavy, for no matter how insistently she told herself that she was being ridiculous, the fact was there, and there it remained. She had fallen for Finbar.

114

'I'm sorry,' she said. 'I really can't seem to do anything right, can I?'

'No.'

'I need some sleep, that's all.'

'Quite.'

'Look, let me just go back to the hotel and get my head down for a couple of hours. I'll be all right.'

'So you keep saying. It's becoming rather a bore.' Finbar's mouth was taut.

'OK, OK,' Rosanna sighed. 'Well, I've apologised. That's it. I can't keep on saying I'm sorry.'

'Quite.'

'Oh God, this is ridiculous.' She threw up her arms in exasperation, then turned her back on him. He didn't bother to speak again.

✳ ✳ ✳

After lunch Finbar ordered them to gather up their swimming gear and took them to the Hotel Etap to relax by their excellent pool. Mike took over the role of being very protective, and would not let Finbar near Rosanna. In any case, Finbar announced that he had things to do, and ordered them all to meet at a restaurant along the corniche for dinner at eight o'clock.

It was not until a waiter came up to the pool, proclaiming that he bore a message for a Mr Bloxham, that the gang realised the Professor had disappeared once more.

'The rascal!' Mike was amused. 'I could have sworn he would have let me in on anything he had going on here.'

Rosanna didn't agree. 'The more I get to know him, the less I feel at ease with him.'

'I know what you mean,' agreed Joey.

'I get the feeling he's not quite straight.'

'Just your vivid imagination, old girl,' Mike told her. 'Professors are all like him — behaving like little boys let out of school, when they get the chance to let their hair down.'

'He hasn't got enough hair to let down!' commented Joey, with a grin.

The waiter's face wore a worried frown. He had a piece of card on a silver tray.

'What's it all about?' Mike demanded. 'I'm the Professor's friend. If you have a message for him, you can leave it with me.' The waiter's eyes narrowed a fraction; he did not care for Mike's tone. 'It could be important, for God's sake. Give it to me.'

Mike reached out and took the card. Rosanna saw that it bore an address in Arabic. The waiter stared down his nose with thinly-disguised contempt as Mike turned it over and shook his head in exasperation.

'It's in Arabic,' he said. 'I can't read it.'

'It is an address, sir,' the waiter told him smoothly. 'A taxi would no doubt take you there, if you wished to go instead of your friend.'

'Do you know why the Professor is wanted at this address?'

The fine eyes remained bland. 'I know nothing at all, sir. It is not my business to know anything.'

Mike tapped the card on his chin.

'OK, my friend. Just you leave this little card with us. We'll see that he gets it.'

'It is not my business to give you the card, sir. The card is for Professor Bloxham —'

'I said I'll deal with it.'

'But —'

'Didn't you hear me? Push off!'

'As you wish, sir. It is not my business to prevent your interference in your friend's business.'

Chapter Seventeen

The taxi took them to a tumbledown backstreet edging on the eastern desert. People watched them suspiciously from doorways as they clambered out onto the track of hard-baked mud.

'Do you wish me to wait, sir?' The taxi-man didn't look at all delighted with the prospect. He sat adamantly in the driving seat, refusing to step outside, as if he thought the car might be stripped down the minute his back was turned. In the circumstances they thought it would be most imprudent to let him go.

'Are you sure this is the right place?'

The driver pointed to one of the hovels.

'What on earth has Monty been up to?' Mike wondered. 'He has some choice friends.'

'Too late to back out now,' said Joey. 'We're here, so we might as well find out what it's all about.'

'Supposing he's angry? Supposing he doesn't appreciate our interference?' Rosanna gnawed her lip. She was thinking to herself that it was not yet too late at all, and that they should clear off before it was.

'Oh shut up, Rosie, there's a good girl. Serve him right for giving us the slip. Come on — once more unto the breach!'

They approached the open doorway the driver had indicated. Before any of them had a chance to call or knock, a figure appeared out of the gloom and stood staring at them, his eyes screwed up against the sunlight.

Rosanna stiffened. Involuntarily she put her hand on Mike's arm.

'Mike, you know who that man is! It's Hassan, from the Museum.'

He came out to meet them, a servile smile cracking his features, which were still just as unpleasant as she remembered them.

'Miss March, my dear Miss March ...' He was beaming over his outstretched arms. 'What an unexpected pleasure. I had not thought to meet you again — but, of course, the Professor —' He stopped and looked past them at the taxi. 'But where is the Professor, my dear? I was expecting ...'

'We've come on his behalf,' said Mike curtly. For once Rosanna was quite grateful for Mike's habit of dealing brusquely with people.

'I see.' Hassan looked him over. 'Well, I suppose if that is what the Professor wishes — who am I to complain? You have the money?'

'Money?' Joey spoke without thinking. Rosanna moved swiftly to cover up.

'It is possible that we have the money. It all depends.'

'I trust I have not come all the way here for you to waste my time,' Hassan said angrily. 'The Professor knows that if he hesitates this time —'

'What have you got?' Mike snapped. 'We don't want to spend any more time in this dump than is absolutely necessary.'

'Show us the stuff, and we'll do the deal!' demanded Joey.

'Show me the money first.'

Mike patted his pocket and laughed. 'Out here, in the open?'

Hassan ushered them into the darkness of the hovel, away from prying eyes. It was sparsely furnished with a mattress, table and chairs, and a couple of stout trunks that served as cupboards. A rather garish portrait of President Mubarraq looked down on them sternly, unsmiling.

118

'Well, what have you got?' Mike had really entered into this game.

Hassan shuffled amongst some bits of newspaper in a box on the table and produced an object wrapped in cloth. He put it on the table in front of them. When Mike reached out, Hassan moved swiftly to stand in front of it.

'The money?'

Rosanna wagged her finger reprovingly. 'Let's see what you're offering, Hassan, then we'll discuss what it's worth.'

Hassan faced her with furious, glittering eyes. 'There is no discussion!' he shouted. 'The Professor knows the deal. No discussion!'

'OK, OK — don't blow your lid,' Mike intervened. 'Give us that thing, and let's have a look at it.'

Hesitantly Hassan allowed Rosanna to take the mysterious object from his grasp. It was a slim parcel, over a foot long. Joey peeped excitedly over Rosanna's shoulder as she began to unwrap it. The cloth was in strips, and bits caught and tangled as her fingers fumbled with it. She was more nervous than she cared to admit.

Hassan never ceased to glower at them. 'Hurry up!' he hissed. 'Your taxi will be attracting much attention.'

'Keep cool, keep cool.' The last layer was a single piece of cloth that came away easily. They found themselves staring at something that looked like a thick black stick, perhaps made of ebony. What caught the eye most were the four bands that encircled it, the proud metal gleaming in the dim light. Gold. Four bracelets of pure gold, two of them set with amethysts, turquoise and carnelian.

Then they realised that the bracelets were not just being displayed on an ebony stick. Rosanna was holding in her hands a mummified arm.

Flooded with revulsion, she shrieked and dropped the ghastly thing on the table.

'Oh God, Mike! Oh God!'

Mike's realisation had come only a second behind hers.

'Where did you get this?' he demanded. Hassan had already snatched up his trophy again.

'Ask no questions!' he shouted. 'Just give me the money, and take it.'

'No way, Mister. No way!' Mike started to back towards the door, and Rosanna followed. 'That loot must be red hot. We're not touching that!'

'Are you crazy? The Professor —'

'Forget it!'

They began to run for the taxi. Hassan charged after them, his furious cries leaving them in no doubt of the trouble and expense he had gone to in order to acquire this prize for Professor Bloxham. Was he now to go unpaid, and leave his men unpaid? What could he do with the arm, and the treasures? He had no other outlet for this very special job, as the Professor knew very well ...

They weren't listening; they were hurtling towards the amazed driver, shouting at him to get them out of there fast. Hassan was upon them while they were still wrestling with the door handle. Mike pushed Rosanna into the cab and flung himself in after her, but Hassan managed to grab Joey and pulled him back viciously onto the road.

'Give me my money!' he shrieked.

Joey flailed like a windmill, and broke free. 'Get in!' Mike yelled, leaning out and hauling him into the cab. The driver didn't need any instructions. Even while the door was still hanging open he accelerated furiously, sending his vehicle screeching up the dirt street, scattering children, goats and chickens. Hassan was left stamping his feet with rage, waving the blackened remains of the ancient arm, and calling down curses upon them as they sped away.

* * *

Dinner was served on the banks of the Nile, where the tall palms swaying and the silver moonlight shimmering across the water took the edge off Rosanna's jangled nerves. Rosanna, Mike and Joey hugged their secret to themselves, and quietly watched the Professor.

'Have you said anything yet?' Rosanna whispered.

Mike shook his head. 'I'll have to, of course. That waiter at the Etap may have already told him that we took the card. This is serious stuff, Rosie, old girl.'

'D'you think I don't know it? I wonder what he'll do?'

'I should think he'll go berserk.'

The Professor, for once, had chosen not to attach himself to Mike; he was eating sombrely at the far end of the long trestle, next to Finbar. He seemed very preoccupied and glum. Probably wondering what had happened to his mummified arm, Rosanna thought. Hassan was bound to come looking for him, and then the cat would really be out of the bag.

She watched the people strolling along the Boulevard, families with small children out late, lovers. She glanced down the table and caught Finbar staring at her. His eyes were hostile.

Rosanna, Mike and Joey left Finbar with the Professor and joined the Springer girls on a walk through the town, pausing to haggle in the bazaar. They bumped into Saud on his patrol. He made a considerable effort to impress them, shepherding them about the streets, and finally taking them back whispering and giggling to the Hotel Panorama just before midnight. They ran smack into an irate Finbar, who had been waiting up for them.

'Are we the last ones home?' asked Bertice sweetly. Finbar ignored her; he simply called to Muhammad that he could now lock up and get to bed.

'Might I remind you that it's our special treat — the donkey ride to the Valley of the Kings — tomorrow,' he said icily. 'We'll have breakfast at four o'clock.'

'That's crazy!' wailed Joey. 'We're exhausted. We need a lie-in!'

'Your problem, I'm afraid,' Finbar told him, with a complete lack of sympathy. 'We have to be there by dawn. By ten o'clock the Valley is a furnace. And believe me when I say furnace.'

Rosanna looked at her watch. Oh God, she thought. She took her key and made for the stairs. Finbar followed her.

'You will insist on being a bloody fool, I see,' he commented harshly. 'You could have been resting.'

Mike was between them immediately.

'Stop pushing her around, O'Neill,' he said. 'OK, you're the courier, but that's it. Nothing else. How can I get it across to you that you're not wanted around here?'

Finbar faced him, tight-lipped. It was a good job they were all so exhausted. Rosanna could see that they were longing to take a swing at each other, but were controlling themselves. Just.

'You've got through,' Finbar said after a moment. 'Loud and clear. Good night!'

He made it sound like a threat.

Rosanna lay on her bed, unable to sleep. The night was full of sounds, disturbed dogs, Egyptians talking — apparently everyone except tourists sensibly slept during the baking heat of the day, and kept busy all night.

Not wanted around here, Mike had said to Finbar. Rosanna rolled onto her stomach and tried to smother the fierce ache of wanting him that raged inside her. Yes, she wanted him. Even with her mind full of apprehensive thoughts about the Professor and the wretched arm, she longed for Finbar to want her.

Chapter Eighteen

It was still dark when they were introduced to their mounts. Some faces were a trifle grim, for Finbar had informed them that they would be spending over two hours in the saddle, and those who had never ridden before were very apprehensive. The Professor had passed up this treat, and was going to join them later the easy way — by taxi.

Fortunately the first part of the journey was on flat land, through the fields, which gave the novices a chance to get the hang of it. When the donkeys began their hazardous climb up the steep mountainside, Rosanna was grateful that they were not on foot, for the going was rough and littered with sharp white rocks. She felt sorry for her donkey, which began to sweat fiercely.

At last they saw before them the towering mound of natural rock that presides over the Valley of the Kings, the necropolis of Luxor. Now they were forced to dismount, for the descent was a painful scramble down a very steep scree slope, where some helpful Egyptians had stationed themselves at strategic points to check the pace of the unwary as they came hurtling past. They also besieged the group with 'antiquities' — scarabs, necklaces of clay beads painted blue, figures made of unfired black silt. Near the bottom the touts were much less persistent, and Finbar explained that the tourist police kept them at bay; the sale of real antiquities was illegal — a fact which had never deterred the villagers from their efforts.

The famous valley was riddled with dark entrance-holes to

tunnels in which the famous ones of Egypt had been laid to
rest. Rosanna was determined to keep away from the Professor as they explored, and this presented no problem, once they
had finished the uncomfortable squeeze around the sarcophagus which held the battered remains of Tutankhamun.

After an hour or so, Rosanna began to wonder what had
happened to Finbar. It was not until she and Mike emerged
panting from the steep grave-shaft of Rameses VI that she
caught sight of him sitting on the edge of the parapet wall
surrounding the rest-house, drinking mint tea.

'I could do with some of that!' Rosanna said.

'You sure?' Mike's raised eyebrow indicated that he was
not at all happy to leave her with Finbar.

To hell with it, she thought; why should I care about either
of them?

Finbar waved to the waiter to fetch her tea. They sat in
silence, not meeting each other's eyes. This is ridiculous,
Rosanna thought; we're treating each other like enemies.

'How do you feel?' he said at last.

'I've been OK since I got the medicine. I'm really grateful.'

'What's this? Humility from the intrepid Miss March?
Can it be that at long last you are learning to appreciate
my tender care?'

'Your *what*?'

Finbar laughed at her outraged face. 'Perhaps that
would be too much to hope for!'

During the next part of the ride, along the clifftop and
down the dangerous track leading to the Deir-el-Bahri
temple of Queen Hatshepsut, Rosanna and Finbar soon got
well ahead of the rest of the party. Finbar burst into song,
his voice echoing back from the hills.

Suddenly, as Rosanna was watching him, she saw his body
jerk to the left. He struggled to keep his balance, but there was
nothing he could do, and to Rosanna's horror he parted company with his donkey, saddle and all. There was a cloud of
white dust as he hit the ground with the saddle on top of him.

'Finbar! Oh, Finbar!' Rosanna was off her own animal in a flash and running to where he lay, quite still, on the rocks. His donkey bucked and kicked out, and then trotted away down the track. Finbar lay, stunned and twisted, mere inches from the cliff edge. He could easily roll over and fall to his death.

Rosanna knelt beside him, her heart in her mouth. He had hit his head and there was a trickle of blood oozing from his hairline. Swiftly she pulled out her water-bottle and, using the hem of her skirt, began to dab the cut clean.

'Finbar, wake up. Wake up, please!' she begged. He groaned, and opened an eye. 'Don't move, Finbar, whatever you do! You're on the edge. Don't move. Just wake up!'

She was holding him by the shoulders.

'I'd rather stay dreaming,' he said softly, starting to sit up.

'For God's sake, Finbar, don't play around now. We could both go over.'

'You could be right,' Finbar said, feeling his head. He stood up carefully, and picked up his saddle. His donkey had stopped fifty feet down the track. 'Wait until I get my hands on Abu Samil. He should have made sure the donkey-keeper had all these girths properly checked.'

He helped Rosanna back onto her donkey, and then led the way forward to catch up with his own mount. Instead of fastening the saddle back on, he rode bareback, holding the saddle in front of him. When they got down, he flung it at the donkey-keeper, swearing at him angrily.

The old man shouted back, just as vehemently. He assured Finbar that Abu Samil had reminded him of his duty, and he had checked the girths while Abu Samil watched. Together they pulled the saddle over, and looked at the straps. Finbar went very thoughtful.

* * *

Back across the Nile, the explorers had the afternoon free, and were supposed to make their own arrangements for food and entertainment. Rosanna knew that the moment of her confrontation with the Professor, and possibly with Hassan as well, could not be put off much longer, but she was going to postpone it for as long as possible.

The girls were going to the bazaar, and Joey was whining that he wanted to go back to the Etap for more swimming. Mike agreed to take him, but naturally wanted Rosanna to go too. She was praying that Finbar would come across, but he had not said anything. In fact, once his official duties were over, he did not speak to her again. She hung around until the girls started up the river bank in the direction of the bistros, then realised dismally that if she did not make a move soon she would be left on her own. That idea did not appeal to her, so reluctantly she began to trail after them.

'Rosanna!' Only one word, but it stopped her in her tracks. 'It's no use your running away from me.'

'I'm not running.'

'Seems to me you are. But I'm going to stop you.'

'Oh?' Her heart was zinging with a hope that she dared not show. Finbar came closer and grabbed her wrist.

'Come on,' he said abruptly. 'Let's go on the river. Just you and me.'

He began to pull her in the direction of the landing-stage. It wasn't exactly what she had had in mind, but the prospects were exciting.

They reached the grassy bank at the edge of the Nile without speaking. Finbar had friends on the waterfront, and a Nubian answered his wave and shout by bringing a small boat with an awning up to the bank. It was as they were teetering across the gangplank that Rosanna heard Mike and Joey shouting after her.

Finbar pulled her into the boat. 'They're too late,' he said. 'You're with me now.'

'There's plenty of room if the others want to come too.'

'We don't want them!'

'But I —'

Finbar said something very impolite, and shouted to the boatman to cast off quickly. The Nubian saw the boys bearing down on them and jumped to it with amazing alacrity. The rope was off and they were away into the stream, leaving the boys fuming on the shore. Finbar smiled darkly.

'Rosie!' Mike was shouting. 'You've let him hijack you! Where are you going?'

'I'll be back soon!' she called.

'Not as soon as she thinks!' Finbar shouted back, enjoying his moment of triumph. 'Don't bother to sit there waiting.'

The small motor began to chug them upstream against the current. The boat had a two-man crew. Rosanna and Finbar stretched out on tattered mattresses in the shade under the awning, while one man worked the tiller and the other treated them to a Nubian love song.

'I suppose you know where we're going?' Rosanna asked, lazily. She rolled over so that she could look at Finbar.

'A little island I know,' he said. Rosanna wished his face was not so grim. She smiled at him, tentatively.

'You *have* hijacked me,' she murmured.

'Do you mind?'

'No,' she said, 'although I have a feeling I may regret it later.'

Finbar made no comment, but stood up and flung off his clothes until his swimming trunks were all that remained. His physique was superb, Rosanna thought, brown and muscular like an athlete's. She had just realised, to her embarrassment, that she was staring at him, when he did a neat dive into the Nile and disappeared. She leapt up in alarm, but the Arab laughed.

'Not to fear for Mister Finbar,' he said, patting her arm. 'He good swimmer. All the boat people know him. We take him out often.'

'With his girlfriends?'

The Nubian laughed.

'He likes to swim. You see. Watch behind.'

127

Rosanna looked at the stern of the boat, where he was pointing. Suddenly Finbar bobbed up and grabbed the end of the long rudder, and heaved himself up on it. He climbed up it and threw a leg over the side of the boat, and the Nubian helped to haul him in. Rosanna paled when she thought of what might have happened if he had missed the rudder, as the current was so strong.

'That's better!' Finbar said, as he rubbed his hands across his chest and down his thighs to brush off excess water, before dropping back onto the mattress again.

'Hey, watch it!' Rosanna cried. 'You're soaking me!'

'Is that so?' Suddenly he rolled right over and took her in his arms, his wet body pressing her into the mattress.

'Get off, you idiot!' she shrieked, wriggling furiously. The Nubian at the stern said something that sent the other into gales of laughter. Finbar laughed too, and let her go.

'Time for tea, Miss March?' he said, primly. Rosanna sat up, blushing. Tea was a word the Nubians knew well, and they soon had flames under a kettle of carcadet on the small wooden deck.

* * *

They lay flat on their backs, gazing up through the green lattice of palm and banana leaves at the dazzling sky, while the Nubians sang under a tree at the water's edge, and two fishermen balanced in a small rocking boat and threw their round nets.

'Finbar,' Rosanna said dreamily, 'why have you suddenly decided to be nice to me?'

'Have I? I hadn't noticed any sudden change.'

'You've started — well — looking after me.'

Finbar rolled onto his side and leaned over her, and stroked the side of her face with the flower end of a piece of grass whose stalk he had been chewing.

'You gave yourself away this morning,' he said, softly.

'You told me everything I wanted to know.'

He threw away the grass stroked her cheek with a very gentle finger. A wild tide of longing surged through her.

'What do you mean?'

'Perhaps I was only dreaming. I seem to remember a certain voice crying "Finbar — oh, Finbar".'

'I thought you were seriously hurt, you idiot! I thought you might go over the edge and kill yourself.'

His hand had dropped to her shoulder, and he stroked her neck with his thumb.

'I'm not such an idiot as you think,' he murmured. 'Until this morning I thought you'd decided to go for Cooper, but since you've obviously changed your mind, I'm not going to waste my chance again.'

Rosanna flung his hand off and sat bolt upright, forcing herself to fight off tears. To her slight satisfaction, at least Finbar looked surprised.

'I'm afraid you've got me all wrong, Mr O'Neill. I have *not* for a moment tried to encourage Mike, nor do I intend to play around with you.'

'Rosanna, you're fighting me again.' He ran his finger up and down the back of her arm.

'What do you expect, if you treat me like dirt?'

'I'm not treating you like dirt.' He wasn't. He was caressing her as if she was a precious, fragile treasure, dear to his heart.

Rosanna's conscience tormented her. He was simply playing her along so that he could add her to his list of female conquests.

'Please, Finbar — don't do this to me. I — I —'

He groaned and rolled over, then stood up, glowering.

'Where are you going?'

'I'm taking a walk. Stay there.'

Rosanna sat up miserably and watched the fishermen throwing their nets.

Finbar came back eventually. He looked sheepish. He was carrying flowers.

Chapter Nineteen

They had dinner alone in the open air along the Nile Boulevard. Rosanna thought she had never seen anything so beautiful as the glimmer of the moonlight across the water, nor heard anything so romantic as the dance music drifting from the deck of a Nile steamer. She knew there would be trouble later. Finbar was skipping his duties. He ought to have taken her back to join the others at the place he had arranged. Rosanna knew exactly what they would think, and she didn't care.

'What do you make of our Professor?' she asked, her thoughts having travelled from guilt at deserting the gang to a more serious guilt at not having told Finbar what had happened the day before.

'Instant dislike,' he replied without hesitation. 'Why?'

'I've got something I must tell you,' Rosanna burst out, all in a rush. 'I think it's important. I should have told you straight away, but —'

'It can't beat what happened to me. That bloody fool.'

'Who?'

'The Professor. Isn't that who we're talking about? I followed him.'

'What?'

'I suppose I ought to tell you my story, eh?'

'But Finbar —'

'I owe it to you to trust you, Rosie. As a matter of fact, I've had my suspicions about our dear Prof for quite some time. He's really *too* eminent to be on a trip like this at all. So I decided that the next time he slipped off on the quiet I'd be right there behind him, keeping my eyes open.'

'So you know where he went while we were at the Etap?'

'Exactly. I saw the waiter take a card for him off a chap at the door, and I managed to get a glance at the address. That was enough to ring alarm bells in my mind. No self-respecting academic would have friends in that part of town unless he was involved in real skulduggery.'

'Really?'

'I know Luxor, Rosie. That particular area is notorious for vice of all sorts. And so was the house he actually went to.'

'He didn't go to the address on the card, then?' she asked innocently.

'No. He probably would have done, but he never got that card. He'd already gone through to the street before it was brought in. I wanted to see where he was heading, so I didn't bother to call him back. Incidentally, that reminds me — I've got to track down what happened to that card.'

Rosanna turned crimson. Finbar didn't notice, but carried on sipping his drink thoughtfully.

'We ended up in a very unsavoury dive, which turned out — surprise, surprise — to be a house owned by one of Abu Samil's relatives. An uncle.'

Rosanna sat up straight. 'Not — not his uncle Youssef, by any chance?'

Finbar frowned. 'Don't tell me you happen to be a close friend of Uncle Youssef.'

'I'm afraid so.' He looked quite startled. 'Tell your story first, please, Finbar — because when I tell you mine I've a nasty feeling you're going to hit the roof.'

'Oh God, I don't like the sound of that.'

'Please, Finbar.'

'Well, as I said, I followed him to this house, and saw him welcomed by an extremely ancient man with an oversized jaw.'

'That's Uncle Youssef all right.'

'They went inside, and I hung about trying to make up my mind whether to go in after him or not. Anyway, that's where I slipped up.'

'Why? What happened?'

'The old boy must have spotted me. He came scurrying out and pounced on me — wasn't at all welcoming. I had to use all my charm to soften him up.'

Rosanna grinned, thinking that in that case it hadn't taken much to fool the old man.

'The funny thing was, then he calmly jumped to the conclusion that I was there for the same reason as the Professor.'

'Looking for treasure?'

Finbar hooted. 'God, no! He thought I was after a woman!'

Rosanna was open-mouthed.

'I know. My first thought exactly. Hilarious! If I wanted a girlfriend, old Youssef said graciously, yes, he could introduce me! I was shown into a seedy bedroom, and after a few minutes a small dark woman was shoved through the door and into my arms.'

'What a shock for you!'

'Come, come, Rosanna! Sarcasm doesn't become you. It *was* a shock. And I was doing my best to hear what was going on next door.'

Rosanna couldn't help grinning. Finbar ran his hand through his hair, his face creased in a frown which showed that he was taking it all very seriously.

'Anyway, when she started on at me I told her to be quiet, and tried to make her understand that I was not interested in her. Then she went crazy. Leapt up and shouted.'

'What about the Prof? And Uncle Youssef?'

'Ah. Now we come to it. I asked her if she knew the Prof. Had he ever had contact with Abu Samil or his uncle before? Well, my dear, he certainly had. It turned out that Abu Samil is the real owner of Uncle Youssef's house, and that the Prof has been there on several of his previous trips to Egypt. Sometimes he was quite content just to collect some packages from Abu Samil or his friends.'

'Packages.'

'Exactly. And don't forget that our Prof gave us no indication at all that he already knew Abu Samil. Very suspicious.'

'Treasure smuggling.'

'Or drugs, perhaps?'

'Treasures, Finbar.'

'You seem very sure.'

'Oh, I am. I have my own confession to make to you in a moment, don't forget. But go on.'

'Well, it turns out that our dear Abu Samil has quite a hold over the Professor, including a collection of photographs, highly incriminating. He's blackmailing him.'

'The whole works,' Rosanna said. A few things were beginning to add up in her mind.

'Anyway, I heard sounds of movement, and guessed that the Professor was off again. At this point I charged out and confronted him.'

'Poor Monty.'

'You know, Rosie, I was expecting a lot of bluster, but he just deflated. He was pathetic. He almost begged me not to make any trouble for him. The man was absolutely sweating with fear — started whining about his reputation, his position at the university. I told him it was a little late for that, since Abu Samil could produce those photos any time he chose. He went green. I thought he was going to pass out.'

'He should have thought of that before.'

'Anyway, Uncle Youssef came in and joined in all the noise. I didn't let on what I knew. The old boy seemed to be scared stiff too, incidentally.'

'Ah. Now, that makes sense to me, Finbar. I found him quite nice when I met him. Don't you think it's possible Abu Samil has got some hold over him too?'

'Perfectly possible. Anyway, I gathered there was still a great deal more to find out, but as the Prof seemed about to collapse on me at any moment, I took charge and hustled him out. That's why he was so subdued last night.'

'Finbar — you've put yourself in danger now, haven't you? They're not going to let this lie. Can't you hand them over to the police?'

'All in good time, my sweet. All in good time. We're going to need a lot of proof. And I'd really like to get the Prof's photos back for him, if possible.'

'You're all heart.'

'Yeah.'

Rosanna thought of the times she had been on her own with Abu Samil and shivered.

'What were you going to tell me?' Finbar asked.

Rosanna quickly explained what had happened when she and the boys followed up the address on the card. Finbar listened soberly. He was not at all pleased that she had become involved, nor that he had apparently misjudged completely the character of his 'old friend' Hassan.

'At least neither Abu Samil nor the Professor knows that you know what I've told you,' he said thoughtfully.

'They'll guess.'

'We'll take that chance. I think at the moment it would be best if you just act dumb. Be very sorry that you intruded on his business.'

'I'll try, but it won't be easy to disguise my feelings. Did you know, by the way, that Abu Samil's uncle was a hypnotist?'

'No, I did not. The one — ?' Enlightenment dawned.

'I'm afraid so.'

'And it was the Prof who set that up? Or Abu Samil?'

'I'm not sure. It seemed like both.' Rosanna paused, deep in thought. 'Do you think it was one of Abu Samil's men who planted that ka on me?'

'I don't think that's something we can take light-heartedly, Rosie,' Finbar said after a moment. 'I'm afraid this business could be pretty sinister.'

Rosanna waited for him to explain.

'Do you remember we were joking, back in Cairo, about the

sacrificed man? Well, I wasn't joking. In fact, when they found that man's remains, they said there was a Horus-ka on his body. And there have been others. A few years ago a man was found with his throat cut, wearing a Horus cartouche round his neck. Last year they found bits of another dismembered body, and a golden hawk statue was embedded in the heart. It caused quite a stir. They were called the "Horus murders".'

'But surely Horus is on the side of good, not of that kind of evil!'

Finbar sighed. 'It's never that straightforward,' he said. 'Horus isn't simply "good". He's the life-force — and the life-force, like any other force, can be used for good or for evil.'

'All the bodies — were they all men?'

'Yes. Just like the old fertility sacrifices. Virile men chosen to represent Horus-Osiris.'

'Never a woman?'

'Not as far as I know.'

'Then why give a Horus-ka to me?'

'That's what I've been trying to figure out. Virgins aren't much good to a fertility cult. However, they do have one use.'

'Do tell me.'

'In ancient times, they drowned a virgin at the first rise of the flood waters each year — the Bride of the Nile. Nowadays, I doubt that's a danger. But ...' His voice trailed off.

'But what?' Something in Finbar's face set Rosanna's spine tingling with alarm.

'But there are other ways of becoming the bride of the god. In the Horus cult, virginity is the prime requisite for a sacred marriage. I think someone was urgently looking for a suitable candidate, and decided to use you.'

The cold clutch of fear gripped Rosanna's stomach. She couldn't believe he was serious.

'How?'

'Probably hoping to get you pregnant with a new little Horus-representative for them to use later. The bearer of a living ka.'

'They couldn't!' Rosanna cried indignantly. 'How could anyone hope to get away with that?'

'If you did disappear, you certainly wouldn't be the first lady tourist to do so. There was a case in Aswan only a few years ago, and lots more in the past. I'd be in deep trouble, of course.'

'Trust you to think of that.'

'The official story on that last woman was that she'd ignored the warnings and gone off the beaten track on her own, fallen into an excavator's ditch, and simply died of thirst and exposure. They didn't actually find her body until two years after she'd disappeared.'

'Two *years*?'

'Precisely. And in that time she could have been used for all sorts of things — including bearing at least one Horus-child for the priesthood to use.'

'You really are serious?'

'I've never been more serious.'

'If I *was* intended for a ritual marriage,' Rosanna said, trying to pull her thoughts together, 'they'd have to provide me with a lover. I suppose you're full of suggestions about that, too.'

Finbar's eyes narrowed. 'I think they were intrigued by the possibility of using Mike Cooper. You told me the lover in your dreams was called Menkheperre. Haven't you noticed the similarity of the names? But then, I think, they began to realise that there was more going on than they had anticipated — that you were already linked to Egypt and Horus in ways they hadn't dreamed of.'

'Oh, Finbar —' Rosanna shuddered. 'I told Abu Samil, that day at Abydos, that since I came to Egypt I'd been having these dreams —'

'Hence the visit to Uncle Youssef, to find out the full story ... I wondered what Abu Samil was really up to. I wish you'd never gone there, Rosie. I can't help feeling that, sooner or later, that little incident is going to have serious consequences.'

'But *Mike* doesn't think he's a reincarnation. No, Finbar, this is all crazy.'

'Is it? Group reincarnation is no more fantastic than that of an individual. If you were Nilufer, perhaps he was Menkheperre. And when I began to move in on you, they thought that would spoil their plans and decided I should be eliminated.'

'But Mike didn't get a ka-statue. I had that.'

'He may have had something planted on him. It doesn't have to be as obvious as a golden hawk.'

'Oh God, Finbar, there was a funny incident he told me about in Cairo. He was followed by a man who kept trying to touch him. Maybe he did plant something ... Oh, Finbar,' Rosanna whispered. 'I did feel drawn to Mike at the start of this trip. I quite fancied him, until —'

'Until I took away the ka.'

'Yes.'

'And now you've transferred all that feeling to me?' He laughed. 'Don't worry, Rosie, my feet are firmly on the ground. I have no intention of being polished off by Abu Samil and his merry men, or taken over by something nasty from the past.'

'But if you're right — it isn't simply the past. It's a past breaking through into the present. Oh, Finbar, we *must* go to the police now. They tried to kill you!'

'I can't prove it. It was an accident. My girth snapped.'

'You don't believe that. You know it was tampered with.'

'I've only hunches and suspicions. The police might well conclude I'd lost my reason.'

Rosanna frowned. 'What about Hassan and the arm? And the jewels? And your business with Youssef?'

'We've got to get some solid proof. The Professor's not going to admit anything. He's too scared.'

'I'm frightened too, Finbar.'

He took her hand and kissed it. 'Don't worry, princess,' he said. 'I'm not going to let them kill me, or have you. I'll get you safely back to England if it's the last thing I do.'

* * *

They walked back, arm in arm, along the corniche. Back at
the hotel the others were having a party. Muhammad had
rounded up some friends, including two of the waiters from
the Etap, and the Springer girls were dancing to the music
provided by Joey clinking a stick between two bottles, Mike
hand-drumming on the table, and some hearty Nubians
singing a chorus-song. They welcomed the truants back to
the fold, and pulled Finbar into the dance. Rosanna was
amused to observe him humouring them — he actually
seemed to be enjoying himself.

Mike edged her to the far end of the room.

'Looks like I've lost, then?' he said.

'Don't be a bad sport, Mike. It just happened, that's all.'

'Like hell!'

'Oh, come on —'

'I didn't like him before, and this certainly hasn't made
me any fonder of him. Why did you string me along, Rosie,
if you wanted him?'

'I'm too tired for this, Mike. Like I said, it just happened. Don't get huffy. After all, the whole trip will be over
in a few days, and we'll go back to our real lives and never
see each other again. What's the point in spoiling what we
have left by bad feelings?'

Even as she said it, her heart began to ache. It was quite
true. It was highly unlikely that she would ever see any of
them again. Abu Samil had called this 'time-out-of-time'.
Soon it would vanish, and reality would close in.

Finbar found her talking with Mike and broke it up.

'Sorry, pal,' he said. 'It's bed-time for Cinderella.'

'But —'

Finbar moved between them. 'I'm putting this girl to
bed,' he said firmly. 'She's been ill, remember? Then I'll be
back to see that you all get some sleep. It will be a hard day
tomorrow.'

138

At her door, Rosanna boldly put her arms round Finbar's neck.

'It's been quite a day. G'night, Finbar.'

He gave her the longest, sweetest kiss she had ever experienced.

＊ ＊ ＊

I pull the door open, just a chink. I have to find him. How can I rest until I find him? Ah — this foul smell! This sickly mix of sweat and dung and incense — and something else: the horrifying reek of flesh long dead, flesh putrefying despite the attention of the embalmers. I feel sick.

There is no sign of the morticians. I push the door open and slip inside.

The state of the room is appalling. Outside, where the relatives come — the customers — the office is kept neat and clean, the hard floor swept, the jars of spices arranged for public display. In here, the walls run with human grease, the floor is smeared with blood, excreta, entrails. There is a grey-white mess in the corner.

For this is not the mortuary to which the last remains of priests or pharaohs come. This is the common vat, the place of preparation for untold thousands who hope to be buried at limited expense, but decently, as best they can. I never thought I would enter such a place. No member of the House of Rameses ought to consider such defilement.

But Menkheperre has gone and not come back. There is no warrior's body to be wept over in honour, encased in jewels, and laid in honourable rest for all eternity. Menkheperre went out into the sun and did not return.

'He has gone for ever,' they said. 'He feared the king's commands. He fled.' I know that none of this is true. No one dares to suggest the truth — that my father lusted for me, his daughter, and that Menkheperre stood in his way. Four of my sisters have already shared Rameses' bed and borne his offspring. Now he wants me.

139

They make up false stories about my love. 'He failed the king,' they say, their voices either shocked or smug. 'He has surely drowned himself in his dishonour.' I cannot believe that he failed. There is no warrior with greater courage in the land. When Rameses faced the Hittites in the great battle at Kadesh, Menkheperre rode in the second chariot. When Rameses was cut off by the plumed enemy warriors, it was Menkheperre who broke through their ranks, who fought beside Rameses until they broke free, who turned disaster into victory.

Each time the sculptors hew the triumph scene on a new pylon, they do it with ironic smiles. The glory for defeating the Hittites always goes to Rameses; but beside him rode the true champion, Menkheperre. How can they suggest that he would dishonour his name?

'Go and search for him,' they sneered. 'Look for his corpse in the common vats, for no respectable House of the Dead will take him in.'

My feet are soiled by the slime on the floor. The air buzzes with flies, so many that I pull my shawl across my mouth and nostrils in case I should breathe them in. I creep to the inner door, and listen.

Yes, the men are inside, in the room of the preparations; I can hear them laughing and talking. I peer through the reed slats of the door.

There are three of them, naked, their dark skins glistening from the sweat and grease. The embalmers are accustomed to the repulsive smell. I have heard that when a family cannot afford to pay, the embalmers simply leave the corpses to steep in natron for thirty days, then hand them back to relatives, little more than skin and bone.

I push the lattice of slats aside and go into the room.

They come towards me, demanding to know what I want, what I am doing there, who let me come in. They are insolent, their red, steaming faces malicious, their eyes lewd. They do not bother to cover their nakedness.

I demand to see the bodies. I offer them money, a pair of gold earrings, a bracelet with carnelian and lapis. They think I am

140

mad. They don't want me to look inside the vats, but I have to see for myself. I have to search. I pay them more.

There are thirty large vats, each one representing a day's work, each vat holding five or six corpses. Getting the new bodies prepared and into the natron is the morning's labour; taking out the bodies in the thirtieth vat at the end of the month's treatment, and delivering them to the relatives, is the afternoon's task.

The supervisor lays his hand on the fine gauze drape on my arm. I pull away, outraged by his touch. He felt the fineness of the material and he raises an eyebrow, but he does not ask who I am, and I do not tell him. It is not important. The only thing that matters is the search.

I insist on seeing inside all the vats. He places the stool against the first huge stone bath and I climb up, bracing myself against the shock of what I have come to see. I peer over the smooth rim. The liquid reaches to the top. It is cold. Five ropes hang over the edge. The supervisor tugs a rope, and something shifts in the tank. I swallow to contain my nausea.

What had been human beings lie hooked in the natron. The heave on the rope arches a corpse chest-upwards out of the natron and a white, empty face breaks the surface, the jaw stretched in an agonised gape. I cannot bear to look at it. The face is dead, but I am frightened the eyes can see me.

I force myself to look.

It is not Menkheperre.

The supervisor asks sneeringly if I have seen enough. I refuse to look at him, his blood-stained leer. I tap the rim of the tank impatiently, and he hooks up the other bodies. One by one. One tank for each day of the month. Five corpses in each tank. I look upon the faces of them all. He is not there.

✳ ✳ ✳

Rosanna sat up, shaking with nausea, and was violently sick.

141

Chapter Twenty

The next day, as they drew near to Edfu — the sanctuary of Horus — Rosanna was both excited and nervous. Edfu was much more to her than just another site on the list. This, after all, was the Shrine of the Hawk, the place where light met darkness, where Horus and his father's evil brother Set met in titanic combat for the mastery of the world.

She took in very little of what Abu Samil was saying. She was frankly amazed at his sangfroid, the complete lack of any indication of what had happened. Perhaps, she thought wildly, his uncle Youssef had not reported what had taken place at his house? But that was ridiculous.

Rosanna forced herself to remember that Abu Samil knew nothing of her conversation with Finbar, of what they suspected. Or did he? He certainly gave no sign, although she felt that her new hatred of him must be stamped all over her face.

The massive girdle wall cut the temple off from the secular world. Dominating the entire space was an enormous statue of Horus the Great Hawk.

The stillness of the grey granite bulk was only a disguise. His eyes, imperious, alert, watched the explorers' every move. If they looked away, the living spirit would stretch its wings and raise its proud beak to the sun. Rosanna tried looking obliquely, from the corner of her eye, but he knew she was waiting to trick him, and did not move. Yet, inside the stone, his blazing eye was watching.

He was the only representation of a living thing which

had not been damaged by the malice of human hands. All around the temple, the faces and figures of the gods had been obliterated, chiselled away with exceptional zeal — reduced to blank smudges that could no longer be identified. They said the Christians and Muslims — who disapproved of idol-worship — had done it. Rosanna wondered.

As they crossed the courtyard, screwing up their eyes against the blinding sun, the muezzin began to call the Muslim faithful to their midday prayer in the village. The fervent cries to Allah reverberated round the Court of Offerings. Rosanna felt humble in the presence of their faith, but Abu Samil was obviously irritated.

'They boast of their ancestors,' he snapped, 'but live only to disgrace them!'

'You are intolerant, Abu Samil.' There was tautness in Rosanna's voice.

'Why not? They should temper their pride with knowledge of their limited power. Let them keep behind their wall, and not interfere!'

'You sound very threatening.'

'No need,' he grinned maliciously. 'They see the falcon, and they fear. Yes, still they fear — after all these centuries.'

'What do they fear?'

'It is not knowing what they fear that makes them afraid.'

Mike asked Rosanna to photograph him patting the Hawk. She wasn't sure whether the Hawk benignly humoured him, or whether it was poised to tear out his throat.

She waited until all the others had entered the Hypostyle Hall, then timidly reached out her own hand and stroked the smooth bulge of the Hawk's chest.

Ancient words moved in her mind.

'Behold me,' she whispered. 'I have come to you without sin, without guilt, without evil — I have given bread to the hungry, water to the thirsty, clothing to the naked — rescue me, protect me —'

She pressed her hand against the stone feathers, feeling

143

the warmth, feeling — almost — the beating of a proud heart. The haughty expression had not changed, of course; but she knew the Hawk was protecting her, had chosen her.

She wanted to be alone. She found a staircase leading up to the top of the great pylon. No one stopped her. The guides had all gone away for their noon siestas, or perhaps their prayers. Up and up, through the darkness where bats skittered into crevices, and out into the crushing, searing heat.

Below her spread the Court of the Offerings, the outer hall where worshippers were purified with water, the first vestibule beyond which lay the sacred precincts that pilgrims, in those days, could not enter. She sat on the stone ridge, remembering.

The second vestibule was where they had worshipped the power of fertility, Horus endowed with creative power and Hathor embracing and receiving that which caused life to be. There were the holy rooms, the Room of Spread Wings, the Room of the Throne of the Sun, the Room of the Victor. There, on the flat roof, was the place where the great procession bringing Hathor from Dendera, at the time of High Nile, culminated in her merging in love with Horus. There, in the courtyard below, they celebrated the triumph of light over darkness, of Horus over Set. There, a live falcon was crowned as the living symbol of Horus on earth.

It seemed an eternity ago, yet only yesterday. She held out her empty arms, as if to pull the sun into her embrace, and closed her eyes.

When she opened them, the god was there.

He strode across the flagstones towards her. His body was golden and gleaming, fresh from the oiling.

She felt a new strength, a dark and ancient power, surging inside her, running through her veins like wine. She was the earth, green and fertile, bursting with a million growing things. She felt as if her hands, her very breath, could conjure life out of bare rock and sand. She was the Nile, always changing and always the same, granting food and water and life to all the land and never growing less. She was mother and sister and lover to all the world; she was comfort, and shelter, and desire.

His hand reached out and touched her shoulder.

'Don't turn away,' he said softly. 'Don't you know that you belong to me? You have always belonged to me.'

'As you have always belonged to me,' she murmured.

She no longer knew what she was doing, for the waves of feeling that washed over her. All she knew was that she ached for him, longed to be with him, to be united with him for ever. His touch kindled in her a rapture that filled her eyes with tears and her heart with wonder.

He gazed at her with dark, passionate longing. The sweat shone on his golden brow. He traced the outline of her cheekbone with his finger. She ran her hands over the golden curves of his arms, feeling the blaze of his desire matching her own; she took his head between her hands and bent it towards her, and their lips met.

'We are not dust,' she whispered hotly. 'Oh, my love!'

She belonged to him as utterly as he belonged to her. The strength of their passion, the passion which had lain dormant for so many centuries, gripped and burned her like liquid fire. She raised her head and cried out triumphantly, a wild cry hurled into the brassy midday sky.

Time-out-of-time. It lasted only seconds. In the distance, in the great courtyard, they heard the clatter of the others returning. Finbar stopped kissing her. They had been seen.

Voices and laughter drifted up to the birth-house of the god. Rosanna was still dazed from the golden moment of realisation. Finbar looked at her, and smiled.

'We can't stay here,' he said softly. She looked at him, her eyes full of questions. He did not meet her gaze this time, but covered her hand with his own and squeezed it gently.

'It's time to go,' he said. 'Back to the land of the living.'

Back to reality, Rosanna thought dully. But what was that reality? What was it that had happened to them, or passed between them? Where would they go from here?

Chapter Twenty-One

They arrived at Aswan, on the first cataract of the Nile, just as the sun was setting. When the coach pulled up outside the façade of a posh corniche hotel, it was so superb that they thought it was a joke and waited to move on. Not until Finbar began to hand them down their suitcases could they believe their luck.

All their rooms were on the top floor, facing the river. Rosanna flung everything off, let cold water rinse away the grime, and crashed out on the bed for a blissful hour. When she woke, she soaped and showered again, washed out some clothes and hung them on the balcony, and made tea. Then she slipped on the evening dress she had not worn since Cairo.

At dinner, Finbar was cheerful, polite, friendly to them all. He kept a discreet distance from Rosanna, however, and only looked at her once or twice. She threw everything into returning those glances. Surely he could see how she felt about him? Probably everyone could.

* * *

When Rosanna awoke next morning, Finbar had gone. She had expected to see him at the breakfast table, dishing out information; but he was not there. Neither was Abu Samil.

They were leaving by plane for Abu Simbel, to see the famous temples Rameses had had cut into the cliffs for himself and his wife Nefertari. Authority had been vested in the Professor, who had ordered taxis for the long ride through the dark, deserted streets to the airfield. By the time they set off, it was light.

Two weeks ago Rosanna had been excited at the mere thought of visiting those temples. Now, she viewed the project with more than a little distaste. She had had enough of Rameses and his megalomania.

Throughout Rameses' temple the walls were carved with the usual reliefs: Rameses beating kneeling prisoners over the head with the hilt of his mace, proud Egyptian steeds stamping on the stumbling, wounded horses of the Hittites. Rosanna pitied Rameses, knowing the truth about that battle! The depiction of his victory showed the king in his chariot, with all his outlines carved double. Rameses the Great — double the power of a man, double the courage, double the speed ...

Rosanna smiled a bitter smile. Yes, there had been a double in that battle: the prince, that nobler cast of the Pharaoh. She wondered if the artist had actually etched those doubles deliberately, for that very reason.

What fascinated her most was the façade of the temple, where four colossi of Rameses sat in perpetual contemplation of the sunrise. Flanking the entrance on either side were statues of his queen Nefertari, and below his knees were several of the royal children — his heir, the crown prince Merenptah, and the four princesses who had shared the royal bed.

Four?

Rosanna stared into the faces of her sisters and felt tears prick her eyes. She had known these girls as children, but she did not recognise them. She counted the statues carefully, looking for a fifth girl. There was none.

What strange feelings she had for the man who had been her father. Had he ever loved her? Not enough to forgive her defiance and have her ka-statue placed beside him, where he could reach down and pat her gently on her head. She looked up at his handsome face, almost white against the cobalt sky. It was not the face of the Rameses she had feared. It was her father in his younger, happier days.

The glorious brilliance of the colours in which he had once been painted was gone now. She could read nothing in the calm, blank eyes. But time and wind and sand had not erased the slight smile on his lips. Was it a sneer of contempt for all the mortals who crawled below him? Cynical amusement that no one dared to challenge his word? Or was it wistful memory, the bittersweet memory of that which had once moved him?

Rosanna gazed at the Horus statue over the central door, crowned with the disc of the sun. Nefertari's temple, a little further along, was dedicated to Hathor. The Divine Lovers. Whatever Rameses had been as an old man, he too had once lived as Horus-on-Earth. Perhaps that was why he had built this temple in his declining years — another attempt to hang on to his virility, to draw the strength of Horus into the king-god whose statue gazed out towards the sunrise.

Poor Rameses. He had wanted to remain Horus forever. He had overruled the priests, defied the Heb-sed trial of his vigour, ignored the law which stated that once the king's vital powers began to wane, he must die. He had wanted to live forever — he himself, Rameses the man, and not just the Horus within him. It was a forlorn hope.

Rosanna wished that she could reach him, tell him that Horus, at least, still lived.

* * *

The Nile was like brass — not a breath, not a bubble troubled the surface. The big boulders in midstream were reflected so perfectly that it was impossible to tell where the rock ended and the water began. Even the hot air hung still.

The island of Philae, the Pearl of the Nile, has always been known for its beauty. It is one of hundreds of islands — some no more than granite rocks, grotesque shapes in purple, red and black looking up out of the water; before the building of the Aswan Dam, it stood clear of the river, offering travellers a pleasant spot to rest after working their boats through the difficult passage of the rapids.

Here, Hathor had been assimilated in her worshippers' minds with the goddess Isis, sister-bride of Osiris. It was here, all those centuries ago, that the women chosen and raised to be the brides of the god came to be impregnated by the pharaohs who passed on the sacred seed. Millions of pilgrims came to make their devotions here; everywhere the rocks and temples bore witness to their prayers.

The surrounding mountains stood out jagged and purple against an amber sky, the temples glowed in rose and gold light. She felt that to break the stillness would be a blasphemy.

She made her way to the forecourt of the temple. On the western side was the birth-house, the womb which received the god. Beyond, a small open court led to the sanctuary.

It was lit only by two small windows. There were no guides, no touts, no other tourists. Rosanna sat for a long time near the abandoned altar, watching the swallows flicker in the deepening sky outside, trying to flood her soul with peace. The first stirrings of the night breeze shifted the fringe of reeds.

'Give me strength to endure,' she prayed.

She wanted Finbar to be with her, to hold her hand, to pull her behind a column and kiss her, to send her whole world spinning. Without him, what was Egypt but sand and stones and a resounding emptiness?

Pain knifed through her bones. He had hurt her, but she forgave him. He was a boy, always a boy. She had been Mother since the ages began. Her arms cherished and comforted. The rattle of her sistrum drove away all evil. And she loved. That love swept out everything else.

Tiny wings fluttered in the last light of the sun. The boatmen were calling. It was time to go.

* * *

There was a movement amongst the dark stones.

Rosanna froze. The silence hung like a thick blanket across the sanctuary, but she knew it was a false silence. Something had moved. There was somebody there.

Telling herself not to be stupid, that it must be Mike or one of the others, she stood up quietly. She could feel tension pull her nerves taut. She listened.

He stepped forward and leaned against the doorjamb in a pose of lazy arrogance. Rosanna felt the skin prickle cold along her arms and back. Even in silhouette she knew him instantly. It was Hassan.

'So. We meet again, my dear.' The voice was cold, dangerous, edged with contempt for her helpless confusion.

'What are you doing here?' she asked stupidly.

He laughed. 'Are you not pleased to see me?' He was still leaning against the stone. Rosanna passed her tongue over her dry lips and tried to gauge whether it was possible for her to get past him. Maybe, if she took him by surprise ...

Hassan saw the direction of her eyes, and smiled. He shifted one leg, pushing it contemptuously forward into the space of the doorway, letting her know that her foolish hopes were in vain. He had no intention of letting her get past him.

'It gives me great pleasure to see *you*, my dear,' he said softly. 'You have caused me much trouble, much inconvenience. But we shall soon settle that score, eh?'

'We?' The flood of fear that washed through her drained all power of movement from her. Her heart was pumping and every vein in her body contracting, but she couldn't budge, couldn't even cry out. Another shape had shifted in the growing darkness, behind her this time.

'Who are you? What do you want with me?' She spun round, hearing harsh laughter. Her heart was thudding like a hammer.

'Why, Miss Rose, I could swear that is fear I can hear in your voice. Fear? And you such a brave, cool girl?'

He was standing perhaps ten feet away from her, a shadow that moved in the darkness. Rosanna swallowed; she no longer

150

had any doubts as to who the second person was. She strained her eyes, trying to see him clearly, but all the remaining light was in the doorway and the shrine behind her was quite dark. She stood still, her feet like lead weights, her throat constricted so tight she could not have cried out even if she had tried.

Abu Samil came forward in a rush. His hand caught her arm from behind and he jerked her round to face him. His thick nostrils flared with his heavy breathing, and his face wore a malicious smile, the dark eyes glittering with satisfaction. The bald dome of his head was damp with sweat. His smile deepened.

'Are you really so surprised that you have been struck dumb? Come, Miss Rose, you knew what you were doing when you interfered in our business.'

Rosanna cleared her throat. The muffled choking sound seemed to give him pleasure.

'If you are talking about that day —'

'Be quiet!' Suddenly he jerked her arm savagely, cutting off her sentence. Hope flared in her. Had Mike come back, looking for her? They stood and listened, the three of them bunched together in the shadow.

A shiver ran through Rosanna's body. In the distance, they could hear the sound of the motor-boat starting up. Her eyes went wild with panic and Abu Samil's smile grew even wider.

'Well, well, well,' he said softly. 'So, your friends have left you behind.'

'But they can't have!' she gasped. 'They wouldn't leave without me! It's impossible.'

'Is it?' There was a strange confidence in his voice. 'Hassan, perhaps you would go and look for us, to see if it is so?'

Hassan nodded and heaved himself back through the door. Once again Rosanna got the wild impulse to hurl herself forward, to take what seemed to be her only chance, but Abu Samil was thinking ahead of her. His grip tightened on her arm. They stood frozen in the darkness, his thumb digging into her arm, his hand never slackening its grip for a second. After a few moments Hassan came back and confirmed, smiling, that the launch had indeed gone.

'But — but — it *can't* have!' Rosanna felt faint. She could not believe they would be so stupid as to leave her behind. Unless — unless it was the Professor's doing? Oh my God, she thought. Yes, of course, that was it. The Professor must have known all along that the two men were there, hiding in the ruins, waiting for darkness to fall. Somehow he must have persuaded Mike that it was all right to leave Rosanna there. Perhaps he had managed to convince him that she wished to be alone, to enjoy her poetical reveries in the gathering darkness. Perhaps he had claimed that the boat would come back for her later. Rosanna swallowed. Her nerves were cold wires tightening under her skin.

Abu Samil stood there, gazing at her from under dropped lids, with an appraising, almost clinical look. Rosanna summoned up all her reserves of courage.

'Well?' she said, curtly. 'It won't be long before my friends come back. What do you propose to do with me until then?'

'Patience, my dear.' The smile was a leer. His touch made her flesh creep. 'Are you in so much hurry, after all?'

'Aren't you? You know they'll miss me soon.'

'Perhaps. But by then, Miss Rose, it will be too late.'

'What do you mean?' Hassan was shifting about in the gloom of the temple like a ghost. In his hands he held a length of rope. The hair rose on the back of Rosanna's neck and her stomach muscles tightened sharply as the thought flashed through her mind that they intended to kill her.

She looked round desperately, but there was no way of escape. Hassan twisted the rope in his hands. She was mesmerised by it. When she spoke, her words came out as a whisper. 'Do you intend to hurt me, Abu Samil?'

It was a foolish question. He grinned at her maliciously.

'Whether I hurt you or not depends very much on you, my dear. It depends on how much you decide to co-operate.'

'With you? Never!'

'I am afraid I am not leaving you much choice. The only decision you have to make is whether you wish the experience to be painful or otherwise.'

'Don't touch me!' she yelled. The echo of her voice bounced off the high stone of the temple roof. Hassan moved up swiftly to help his master grapple with her. Between them, they wrestled her across the floor and out into the empty courtyard.

'Where are you taking me?' she gasped. 'What are you going to do with me?'

They were pulling her along as easily as if she had been a child. Desperately, she tried to fight them, but their combined strength held her effortlessly and her feet hardly seemed to touch the ground as they lugged her swiftly through the courtyard, towards the looming edifice that was the birth-house. Blind panic seized her. She screamed and bucked.

It was to no avail. They had her through the portal and into the place where countless queens and princesses of the past, in the name of Hathor-Isis, had received the seed of the god. She screamed again, and one of Abu Samil's hands clamped over her mouth, crushing her lips against her teeth. His other arm was wrapped round her, under her bosom, heaving her straining body against him. The acrid smell of his sweat filled her nostrils. His palm was sticky with sweat, and Rosanna wrenched her head away from him, lashing out desperately.

Abu Samil flung her down with all his force. Her knee smashed against the cold stone, and she pitched forward into the dust, which rose in a thick cloud and set her choking.

She had no time to clear her mouth of it before he was upon her, pressing his weight down on her, forcing her under him. She was vaguely conscious of Hassan watching from the doorway, his face split in a wide smile.

She was on her back with one of her arms twisted up beneath her. When Abu Samil shifted a little sideways, Rosanna wrenched her arm free, but it gave her no advantage. His heavy body pressed her down, so that she couldn't move. One of his hands had seized her wrist and was holding it crushed against the cold stones. His other hand was beginning to grope at her.

Rosanna screamed again and twisted violently, jerking from side to side in a desperate effort to throw him off. Hassan was laughing, a hoarse guttural laugh of pleasure, and offering Abu Samil the use of the rope. Abu Samil hit her hard across the mouth, sending her head back with a crash onto the stones.

'Keep still, you vixen, then it won't hurt you so much!' he hissed.

'You're mad! Mad!' Rosanna shrieked. 'You can't expect to get away with this.'

'You are wrong, my little princess. You thought you could escape me? Now you know better. There is no escape for you. Not this time.'

The choking clutch of terror nearly suffocated her. She went very still. Abu Samil, surprised, lifted himself up on one elbow and glared down at her.

'That is better, my dear,' he growled. 'You have changed your mind?'

She was staring at his face. A river of sweat was coursing down from his forehead, soaking his throat and neck. His eyes were full of triumph, his nostrils flaring like a bull's. In that single appalling second, she knew him — knew the curve of those thick, sneering lips, the cruel glitter of the black eyes. Blood hissed in her ears. A blackness was rising like flood-waters in her body, drowning her, taking away her will to live. She began to slip under. His eyes became huge black pools, filling his face.

She could not speak, could not even whisper. But she knew — even after all those centuries, she had recognised him. He was laughing, a cruel laugh that began deep in his throat and shook his frame. User-Maat-Re, Rameses II. He was there, in the birth-house, and she could not escape him.

Chapter Twenty-Two

As the curtain of unconsciousness closed over her, Rosanna's last bitter thought was that perhaps she would die now, perhaps the shock would kill her. She was almost glad at the thought; at least then all their evil plans would have been in vain.

Even as Abu Samil leaned forward over her body, there was the sound of a speeding engine and Hassan leapt to his feet. He had been crouched down beside them, watching his master's actions with glee. Now his face was a mask of fear as he spun round and ran to the door of the birth-house.

Abu Samil stiffened and looked up, the mad glaze sliding from his eyes. They could both hear shouting. Someone was coming. The boat had come back. In the still air Rosanna's breathing was as loud as sobbing. Perhaps she was sobbing. She was no longer conscious of anything with any precision.

A voice cut through the gloom like a knife.

'Rosanna! Rosie!' It was a man's voice. It had to be Finbar. She was going to be rescued after all. She breathed in deeply, filling her lungs as Abu Samil lifted his weight off her chest.

'For God's sake — where are you? Rosie!'

Relief made her dizzy. She shut her eyes and rolled her head back against the stones. She could hear footsteps clattering in the courtyard. He was coming for her, and by the sound of it he was not alone.

The beam of a powerful torch speared out of the darkness and caught Abu Samil full in the face. He recoiled, as

155

if the light were a physical blow.

But it was not Finbar who stood there looking down at them. Rosanna's heart shrank to a tight lump. It was Professor Bloxham, and in his hand was the gun he had used to kill the snake.

'So. It's you, is it? Well, come in, my friend,' grated Abu Samil, hardly bothering to twist his head round to look at him. 'You could not bear to miss the excitement after all?'

Rosanna gasped in despair. A hopeless tear squeezed from the corner of her eye and rolled down her cheek.

'Just a moment.' The Professor's voice had a new edge to it, a strength. Abu Samil heard the new tone too, and looked up.

'What is the matter, Professor? You are squeamish? Or perhaps you just want a better view?'

'Get away from that girl!' Bloxham's voice was shrill, high-pitched with nerves. Abu Samil laughed.

'Don't be a fool. Hassan, keep this idiot out of the way.'

Suddenly violence erupted in the room as the furious figure of Finbar hurtled through the doorway and onto Hassan, knocking him to the ground.

'He's got a knife!' shrieked the Professor, waving his gun and looking for a target. The two men rolled over and over in combat. Abu Samil dropped Rosanna and struggled to his feet, his mouth pulled back in a grimace.

Knife. The word stirred in Rosanna's consciousness. She turned on her side and groped for her shoulder bag. It was just beyond her reach, where it had fallen when Abu Samil forced her down. She edged towards it until her fingers touched the canvas, closed around the strap and pulled it silently towards her. Her hand slipped down inside, and probed for the tartan souvenir. Yes — it was here. She grasped it triumphantly. In a flash she had it open, and was on her knees with the blade stretched out towards her attacker.

'Don't just stand there!' Finbar shouted to the bemused Professor. 'You've got the gun!'

156

The Professor raised his arm, the gun shaking as he tried to aim it. He was obviously deeply shocked. Abu Samil did not hesitate, but lunged forward and hacked him across the forearm with all his force. The gun shot out of Bloxham's grasp and hit the stones with a crash, skittering across the floor. Abu Samil's next blow sent the Professor stumbling backwards against the wall, blood streaming from his lips.

Rosanna hurled herself at Abu Samil with the knife gripped tight in her sweating hand. The blade glinted in the starlight striking through the birth-house door, and she buried it in him, up to the hilt. He howled with pain and fury. She wrenched the blade out and made ready to stab him again. Blood spurted through his fingers as he clutched his wounded shoulder.

'You damned vixen!' he cursed.

She went for him again. He dodged, and glanced at Hassan; but he was still grappling with Finbar. Shouting to Hassan to save his own skin, Abu Samil took off across the dark courtyard.

Rosanna was shaking like a leaf. She saw no point in giving chase; she turned back to help Finbar. Finbar, however, had no qualms about using Hassan's face as a punchbag, and soon the man collapsed in a helpless, slobbering heap.

'I don't think we're going to have any more trouble from him,' Finbar declared triumphantly. Rosanna threw her arms round his neck and kissed him.

'Oh, Finbar!' she cried, the tears coursing down her cheeks. 'Oh, thank God you came! But where have you been? How did you know — ?'

'It's the Professor you've got to thank,' Finbar said soberly. Rosanna's eyes widened. The Professor was wiping the blood from his split lip and leaning against the wall rather shamefacedly.

'I let the bastard get away,' he muttered.

'Not your fault,' said Finbar cheerfully. 'We know you're not into fist-fights and all that sort of thing.'

'I had the gun in my hand.' He still looked bemused.

'That's a point. Better find your gun. It could come in handy again later. Rosie, kindly stop waving that thing about. You're making me nervous.'

'What? Oh —' She had forgotten the knife. Hair streaming, clothes dishevelled, the bloodied knife still wildly clasped in a rigid hand, she looked like an avenging fury. She folded the blade down and put it back in her bag.

'You've the Professor to thank,' repeated Finbar. 'I finished my business, came out to the landing-stage to meet you all, and discovered to my horror that you weren't with them. Mike gave me some cock-and-bull story that he'd heard from the boatman.'

'So that was it. Abu Samil must have paid him.'

Finbar nodded. 'Anyway, the Professor was listening. He hadn't even noticed your absence up to that point — typical bloody academic. But when he heard about the boatman, his brain was right on the ball. He knew what they were going to do to you, and he couldn't let them go through with it.'

'He knew?'

'Come on, now, be big-hearted. I wouldn't be back here now, saving you from a fate worse than death, if it hadn't been for his courage. He had a lot to lose, you know.'

'So had I!' Rosanna snapped. The Professor hung his head.

'You can hardly call it courage,' he mumbled. 'I am ashamed, my dear, truly ashamed, that I let you get caught up in all this. I'll make it up to you somehow. I just hope that you'll be able to forgive me some day.'

'I'll try,' Rosanna said grimly. She was not in a very forgiving mood. He legs were still shaking, and her whole body was outraged at the thought of what Abu Samil had been about to do to her.

158

Finbar dragged the dazed Hassan to his feet.

'Come on. Let's get this fellow under lock and key.'

A thought froze Rosanna to the spot. Her heart gave a frightening jerk. They had not been thinking about Abu Samil.

'Finbar!' she cried. 'What about Abu Samil? And what about the Professor's photographs?'

'Oh God,' groaned Bloxham. 'Don't tell me *you* know about them, too.'

'Afraid so,' Rosanna admitted. 'But don't worry, Prof. We're on the same side now, aren't we? Looks like I owe you a favour.'

'*I* owe you one,' said Finbar gruffly. 'I nearly lost my best girl.'

'Maybe Hassan knows where the negatives are,' said Bloxham, looking hopeful. They all glared at the cowed Hassan.

'Are you going to tell us the easy way,' Finbar asked him, 'or are we going to have to apply a little pressure?' He jerked the man's arm. Hassan still had enough resistance to spit contemptuously. Finbar slapped him across the face, hard. 'You won't be so high and mighty, my friend, when the police have finished with you,' he snapped.

Chapter Twenty-Three

The next day was an anticlimax. Finbar insisted that Rosanna should stick to her programme of sightseeing and leave him alone to get on with his investigations. With Hassan under lock and key, the Professor was in a very precarious position. Hassan had proved to be extremely talkative, under police pressure. According to him, the Professor had committed virtually every criminal offence known to man, short of assassinating Mubarraq or blowing up the High Dam, and if the foolish authorities did not lock the foreign pig up immediately, it would not be Hassan who was to blame if the Professor rushed out and did those very things.

The police were rather more interested in the parts Hassan and the Luxor underground had played in the sale of treasures. The Professor was not arrested, but he was given a police escort and ordered not to attempt to leave the hotel, pending further investigations.

No one knew what had happened to Abu Samil, but of one thing Finbar was quite certain — it was easy enough, in Egypt, for a scorpion to get under a rock and lie low. Nevertheless, Finbar was determined to find him.

Rosanna did not want Finbar to leave her. She wanted to go with him, but he wouldn't hear of it. He had spent the night at the station with the police and was very irritable. It occurred to Rosanna that he was actually enjoying this little drama, hugging it to himself like a dog defending a bone.

She regarded him soberly. His attitude had hardened

since yesterday. The smile was guarded again, the mouth obstinate. The very last thing she wanted was for him to regard her as a liability.

'OK, fine,' she said, too brightly, probably. 'Off you go and play detective. Don't spare a thought for me.'

'I won't,' Finbar grinned. The flash of disappointment in her eyes must have been terribly obvious, because he laughed out loud.

'Come on, Rosie,' he said softly. 'You've been wonderful up to now.'

'Have I?'

'You don't need me to tell you.'

'But it's rather nice when you force it out.'

'You know,' he said, 'you're very provocative. But I don't want you hanging round me. You might get hurt. You've seen something of what's going on, and been on the receiving end. It's obvious that we can't risk you getting yourself into any more danger.'

'Heaven forbid! You go ahead and be a hero, and leave me to work on my suntan.'

'Rosie!' He wagged a finger at her.

'Well, I can't see why you don't just leave it all to the police. That's the simple answer — which, I suppose, is why you won't consider it.'

'My dear,' he said patiently, 'if we just let our friends the police arrest him, he will be charged with what? Treasure smuggling and its allied offences —'

'Little things like blackmail, extortion, not to mention attempted rape!'

'That will only put him behind bars for a few years,' Finbar snapped. 'You and I know that he is involved on a much deeper level. A level the police won't understand.'

'They understand murder.'

'Where can you find a lawyer who will accuse someone of being taken over by a supposedly long-dead god?'

'Oh, Finbar, be careful!' All of a sudden Rosanna was

161

conscious of a longing to escape, to leap on a plane and be away into the bright blue sky, back to the point where she had come in.

'It's all getting too much for me,' she said. 'I'm getting the feeling that I can't cope with much more.'

'Right,' he said dryly. 'So just you relax, baby, and leave it all to Uncle Finbar. Go back to sleep. When you wake up you'll find it's all been just a nasty dream.'

'Maybe it has.'

'Safer that way,' he said. He took her hand and kissed the ends of her fingers, one by one. A tremor ran right through her.

'Finbar, I'm not safe, and neither are you.'

He put her hand down, irritably. 'We've talked enough,' he said. He ignored the hurt look in her eyes. 'Don't go anywhere on your own. Stay with Mike. I'll trust you not to be silly with him, eh? Stay with him, and you'll be all right. I've got things to do, and standing around talking isn't getting me anywhere. I'll be back tonight.'

'Tonight?' The kick of fear again. She clutched his arm. 'Finbar, where are you going? What are you going to do?'

'Mind your own business,' he said, but not unkindly. He unwound her fingers from his arm. 'Well, do you promise faithfully?'

'Do you really care?'

Finbar looked at her, and she could swear she saw tenderness there somewhere. 'You are my girl now, aren't you? We've got a deal, eh?'

Rosanna did not dare to allow the flicker of hope. She laughed, to hide the raw ache in her heart.

'Sure. For as long as this trip lasts.'

There was a pause. She saw his body tense, just for a second. He didn't need to speak; the mixture of bluff, shame and bravado on his face told her everything she wanted to know.

'OK, princess,' he said.

162

Rosanna stayed with the gang. They took taxis to the granite quarries just south of Aswan, to walk in awe the length of an enormous obelisk which had never been completely freed from the rock, and then admired a huge unfinished sarcophagus and a statue of an Osiris-king half buried in the sand.

Rosanna tried hard to take it in, but all the joy had gone out of her. As soon as they were back at the hotel, she hurried to the front desk to ask if Finbar had returned.

The man shrugged. No one had seen Finbar. He had many friends in the town. No doubt he would soon return, and find his lady.

Rosanna cringed. She got the distinct impression they were laughing at her, knew all about her hopeless relationship. The inscrutable brown eyes of desk-clerks, waiters, and miscellaneous men with brooms had assessed her and marked her up as just one more conquest for Mister Finbar.

She sat disconsolately on a huge green sofa, watching Mike and the Professor play pontoon with his police guards. The sun had gone and the lights were up along the corniche. The manager came to invite them upstairs for dinner. There was still no sign of Finbar. Or Abu Samil.

'No point in waiting,' said Bloxham cheerfully. 'We might as well go on and eat.'

Halfway through the meal an Egyptian came in and signalled to the manager. As he held his arm up, something caught Rosanna's eye. On the middle finger of his left hand was a ring with the same square of black stone that she had seen in Cairo.

She stared hard at him. He was clutching a parcel wrapped in newspaper, tied up with string. The manager went over to him and was given the packet. They conversed a little in Arabic; then the man with the ring went out.

The manager turned the packet over and over in his

hands. He looked worried, embarrassed. He came across to their table. A prickle of fear ran through Rosanna. She told herself to calm down.

'Mr Bloxham, sir,' he said, 'I think I had better give this package to you. You are the father of your group.' They all laughed at that; but in spite of herself, Rosanna could feel tension pulling all her nerves taut.

'Anyone got a knife?' Bloxham asked. Rosanna handed him her penknife and he cut the string.

The newspaper opened, and they found themselves looking at clothing. Rosanna gripped Mike's arm tightly, her face a frozen mask. The shorts and shirt were unmistakable.

'I am very sorry,' the manager said quietly. 'The boatmen brought these in. It is very possible that your Mr O'Neill has met with an accident.'

Rosanna's blood ran cold.

'What are you saying?' Her voice was shrill with panic. 'Where did that man get these clothes?'

'They were found by the Nile,' he said. 'We are very sorry, madam. The police have been informed. We believe there is every possibility that your friend has drowned.'

* * *

Songs of death ring in my ears. The muffled, hollow thud of the death-beat, the drumsticks swathed in leather.

> *I hear one whose name is 'Come'.*
> *It is death, who calls everyone to herself.*
> *She calls and they come, no hesitation,*
> *though they tremble with fear before her.*
> *No man or god sees her approach.*
> *The great are in her hand as well as the small.*
> *No man can keep her away from his loved ones;*
> *she steals the little child away from his mother*
> *more willingly than the old man waiting at the door.*

Face grey with grief, body faint with shock, heart turning to stone. Oh gods, if you pity me, let my heart turn to stone. One foot in front of the other, one step at a time, one breath at a time, inching behind the heaving slaves, and the red oxen drawing the precious burden to the tomb. You red and magic Nile, you who give life to men and cattle, could you not have spared him whom I loved?

> *Oh my brother, my prince, my love!*
> *Let your heart be drunk, be full of love.*
> *Spend the day happy.*
> *Let your heart be at ease night and day, don't be afraid —*
> *what do the years matter that are not spent on earth?*
> *The West is the land of dreaming;*
> *It is I who suffer, I who am left;*
> *I thirst, even though water is at my side!*

Stand him up to face us for the last time. Farewell, beautiful face, beautiful eyes, beloved one. Propped before the yawning gape of the tomb.

> *Awake, O drowned one, taken by the Nile!*
> *Surely your soul lives, for you are strong.*
> *You breathe the air, and go forth like a god!*
> *How noble you are, how mighty your soul!*
> *Your name is immortal in my mouth,*
> *your heart is immortal in my body.*
> *It shall endure while Ra reigns in the sky.*
> *Go in peace, Min-Kheperu-Re.*

Let me touch him, let me hold him one last time. Do not restrain me. See, the dust from my body clings to his fine shroud. You will take the dust with you, my prince, but not my offered self.

I hear the words they have allowed for you, the funeral hymns, the ancient texts. Do I believe them? How can I believe that he whom I have loved has gone?

The priests are bowing, the coffin slides within. It is done. The act of rebirth is complete, a new soul born on the other side.

The family can go home now.

I turn my face to the north wind on the shore.
O let my heart find ease from its sorrow!
O thou great goddess, cover him with thy wings,
protect him, while the stars shall endure!
O darling of Thebes, sit for ever in peace,
with thy face turned toward the north wind,
and thine eyes filled with love.

The sculptor has carved the last lines of the poem on an alabaster bowl. It is the one thing of his they have not buried with him. Such a simple bowl, they overlooked it. But I will hide it, I will keep it safe. I will not let him be forgotten.

They told me he deserted, that he drowned himself in his shame, that the Nile refused him and returned his corpse to the king, a cold and swollen stranger. They would not let me see his body. There was nothing left that was him, they said, nothing that those who loved his soul would recognise; the blank face was no longer his. They would bury him with respect only because of the great prince he once was.

But I saw the Queen's eyes slide away, and a flush of sweat break through the gold-dust upon the Pharaoh's brow. I did not believe them. When did a Horus-warrior ever willingly lay down his spear and run, or feel such shame at life that he would try to slip beneath the flood?

It is the time of Heb-sed; Rameses is old, his body shrivelled like a dried pod, yet still he refuses to let go. He is surely accursed for withholding what he owes to the land. I watched him close the door upon my dear love's empty corpse. His eyes shed no tears. His face was triumphant, satisfied; as if, somehow, the Horus-blood had been shed for him after all.

Cold fingers clutch my throat. The Pharaoh says that my beloved never loved me, that his words were a sham. He says that if I refuse him now, he will wall me up to die. My soul is spreading its wings, preparing to fly. I have to know the truth, quickly, before I close my eyes to day, before I offer my heart to my lost love, that my soul may find him and we may be together through eternity.

I slip away, and go back to the tomb.

I pay the priests. A collar with dark blue porcelain drops, a knife of Hittite iron, a skirt with seven tiers of golden rosettes. A belt of beaten gold and a dagger engraved with figures. Not enough? A chalcedony scarab with falcon's wings, set in a gold pectoral. An alabaster cup shaped like a lotus, inscribed with wishes for the beloved one. Will that not move you?

They unlock the door. Enter the serdab, with its smell of new limewash and incense. Clutch in sweating hands the symbol of the Eye of Horus. I mustn't be afraid. It will protect me from all evil. Gaze upon the piles of offerings, the calm beloved face newly chiselled in haste upon a standard statue, the youth sitting as Menkheperre never sat, stiffly, bolt upright, hands on knees.

Stand shaking beside the stone sarcophagus. Break the seal. Lift the lid. Reach within, caress the mummy case, inlaid with shimmering gold, carnelian, lapis. Steady, steady. Each tiny stone inset with utmost care, as if they had loved him. Below the crossed arms of the prince's image, two lovely goddesses enfolding him with their wings. Draw the fastening bolts of iron and gold.

Now the wrapped mummy. Gleaming white swathes of royal linen, and the glitter of gold and jewels. The priests hesitate, fearing the curse. No curse on one who loved him. What I do is done not to disturb him, but to give him peace.

I nod, and the priests cut through the wrappings.

The truth. Bare. Open. The screaming truth.

A gash across the throat, and a huge wound in the padded breast, over the heart. Plunge my hand into the empty cavity. Empty — there is no heart.

It is not true that he was drowned.

Chapter Twenty-Four

'Drowned?' The Professor spoke for them all. 'What do you mean, drowned? How? Where?'

'It is very unfortunate. What can I say? The police are investigating. There is nothing else that I can tell you.'

'My God!'

'Will they need one of us to — to identify the body?'

The policeman coughed. He looked embarrassed.

'There is no body, as yet, to identify. It has not yet been recovered. You must know that the currents are very strong here. Very swift. Perhaps tomorrow ...'

Hope leapt in Rosanna's heart. If they had not found him, if they only had his clothes ...

'Then surely that means there's a chance?'

'It is unlikely. I am afraid you must face the facts. These abandoned garments surely suggest that Mr O'Neill foolishly went swimming off the corniche. He has not returned.'

Shocked silence.

'It is a terrible thing. Most distressing. But we must be practical,' the manager said. 'Do not worry about your arrangements. Telephone calls will be made, another courier will come from the Cairo office to take you safely to your destinations. In the meantime, I trust you will accept the hospitality of this hotel. Ask for anything you wish. Please do not hesitate. My staff will have instructions and will understand. I am most sincerely distressed on your behalf.'

He bowed and left. They sat round the table, shattered.

'I don't believe this,' said Bertice. 'It just isn't happening.'

Rosanna tugged Mike's sleeve.

'Mike, would you come with me to my room?' she asked quietly.

'Of course.' He stood up and took her arm. 'I guess this has hit you pretty hard, huh?'

'I knew he liked to swim. He was a good swimmer.'

'The Nile's a treacherous river,' said Bloxham, pushing back his chair.

'It's all right,' said Mike, stopping him. 'I'll go with Rosie. You'd better do some arranging with that manager. I'll see you later.'

'I'm coming too,' chipped in Joey.

Mike steered Rosie out of the dining room without another word. When they were alone, she no longer tried to hide her fears.

'Listen. You've got to trust me. Finbar is in terrible danger. He needs our help.'

'What do you mean, Rosie? There's not a lot we can do for him now, old girl.'

'He hasn't drowned! That's rubbish — I don't believe a word of it. It's all a fix, Mike. But he certainly could end up dead if we don't move fast.'

'What are you talking about?'

'Mike, Joey, please listen to me! I know why he's been taken, and I think I know where he's been taken to. We've got to get there in time to save him.'

'Get where? Rosie, will you make sense?'

'To Karnak. Karnak! That's where they'll do it, if we don't stop them.'

'Do what?'

'Sacrifice him.'

'Are you crazy?'

'I'm not sure if I'm going crazy or not. But you know that what happened to me yesterday was real enough. You've got to believe me. We've got to try. Please! Please

169

help me. Can you get a fast car — without telling anyone?'

'I'm not sure I want to help you. This is the darndest thing I ever heard.'

'I'm with you, Rosie! You can count on me!' Joey was right beside her. 'What's the matter with you, Mike? No real guts?'

'Please, Mike — we need your help. We can't do this on our own. Get a car. We've got to save him.'

'I guess you really loved this guy, eh?'

'Believe it.'

'I'll have a word with the Prof.'

'No! Don't tell him. I still don't think we should trust him, Mike!' Joey was adamant.

Mike shook his head, baffled. 'I still think this is a waste of time, Rosie,' he muttered, 'but —'

'Please!' Rosanna hung on to his arm. 'Just do this one thing for me. Just get us to Saud in Karnak!'

'Saud? Don't you think he could be involved too?'

'Oh, Mike, no! Surely not! He was so nice. And he's in the police.'

'Haven't you ever heard of bent police? And he is Abu Samil's brother, after all.'

'Mike, we're wasting time. We can argue about all this on the way.'

* * *

They burnt up the miles along the deserted road in a modern Datsun, and arrived in Luxor just before four o'clock in the morning. Rosanna glanced anxiously at the sky. There was an orange glow on the horizon. Not long until dawn. She was certain that dawn was the crucial time.

'Where to now?'

'The Heb-sed Temple.'

'Wait!' cried Joey. 'If you're right, Rosie, we can't do this on our own. We do need the police.'

'There isn't time! Look at the sky!'

170

Mike leaned forward and told the driver to stop a short distance from the Karnak temple complex.

'What about Saud?' Joey asked. This was the subject they had been avoiding. They looked at each other, not knowing what to do.

'OK.' Mike breathed deeply. 'We'll take the chance. Let's hope this great friendship turns out to be more than just talk.'

He dashed off an urgent note and gave it, with Saud's address, to the driver, telling him to deliver that first and then go straight to the town police. They prayed that the man would take them seriously, that he was not police-shy. They loaded him with baksheesh, and he pulled out, calling down Allah's blessings upon them for their munificence, and swearing that he would not simply leave Luxor and go back home, but would see to their requests immediately.

The taxi roared off with a flurry of dust. They were left, fearfully alone, in the rising light.

'We could do with the Prof's gun,' Mike muttered.

'Oh, Mike!'

They hurried along the dark street towards the looming ruins, stepping carefully where the pavement was in need of repair. Mike found some battered railings, and helped himself to a heavy iron bar which had been broken in such a way as to leave a sharp end, like a spear. It was a rough and ready weapon, but better than nothing.

The place was deserted; the silence was intense, as thick as a curtain, blanketing the ancient stones.

'What now?' Joey whispered.

Rosanna could only be grateful that they were humouring her in what they must have thought was a ridiculous wild-goose chase. She gritted her teeth.

'Keep going. Straight through the big hall. The Feast Hall. I tell you, I know the place.'

The mighty bulks of the pylons reared up like dark mountains, even more forbidding in the darkness than they had been by day. Rosanna, followed by Mike and Joey, nervously began to feel her way past them. A hundred feet above their heads the sky was alive with bats flickering back to their crannies before the break of day.

They crept past the pylons and into the courtyard of the great Feast Hall, like stealthy night-cats, hugging the shelter of the boundary wall. The filter of soft sand underfoot made silent walking.

At the far end of the Feast Hall was the Holy of Holies, the Gate of Heaven, the Gate of Horus Rising. In front of it was the altar stone.

They paused for a moment, their eyes straining against the dark. The dawn air was very still. There was no sound. Rosanna's heart was beating light and fast, her mouth dry. Supposing she had been wrong?

'There's no one here,' said Mike quietly. 'This is madness, Rosie. Madness.'

'We'll wait!'

They crouched in the shadows, waiting.

Something moved beside Rosanna's feet, brushed against her with a soft touch, almost startling her into breaking the silence — until she realised it was only a large temple cat on some secret business of its own. When she stretched out a hand to fondle it, it slid away from her and vanished in the ruins. She took a deep breath to steady the violent beating of her heart.

'I heard something,' Joey whispered.

They ducked down. There was a shuffling, a small scraping sound, then a soft rustle. Whoever was there was obviously not expecting an audience. Mike nudged Rosanna and pointed towards the columns.

A man came out into the open space, a businessman in a smart pin-striped suit. He looked round hesitantly, then struck a match. The spark and flare lit up his face and the sharp reek of Egyptian tobacco wafted to their hiding-place.

'What do you make of that?' Mike whispered. 'One of the staff? He doesn't look like my idea of a villain.'

'He doesn't look like one of the staff either,' Rosanna murmured. 'And why is he here, before dawn?'

They observed him. He seemed nervous, and kept looking at his watch.

'There!' hissed Joey. Another man had stepped out of the shadows to join the first. He also looked quite out of place in those ruins; he should have been in a penthouse office, dictating to secretaries. The two men greeted each other with handshakes and kisses, then stood talking quietly. Rosanna glanced at the sky. It was lightening fast.

Suddenly there were rapid steps quite close by, and they froze. A third man had appeared from a different direction. He passed not a dozen yards from where they were hiding, and they shrank down, flattened into the shadows of the columns. Rosanna's breath came so lightly it did not even shift the grains of pale sand which were sharply in focus beneath her mouth and nostrils. If the man saw them, if he saw them ... But he didn't. They watched his back as he hurried to join his friends, and breathed a sigh of relief.

Soon the courtyard contained more than a dozen well-dressed men, all middle-aged, dignified, and carrying black briefcases. Rosanna, Mike and Joey watched, fascinated, trying to understand what they were seeing.

Then there was a new sound: a gong, a leather hammer beating on brass. The casual talking stopped. The men moved together and looked expectantly towards the Gate of Heaven.

Three men emerged. They were all dressed in white, the two outer figures in long, flowing robes. Bareheaded, naked to the waist, his feet unshod, the man in the middle wore nothing but a pleated white loincloth and a golden Horus-ka hanging round his neck. The outer two were supporting him, as he had considerable difficulty in walking.

The three hidden watchers strained their eyes to see.

'My God,' Mike breathed. 'Is that Finbar?'

It was. Rosanna's nerves were screaming. She knew it. She had always known it.

The gong continued to beat as the three men reached the altar stone.

'Where are the damned police?' hissed Mike.

Finbar was offering no resistance. He seemed to be in a trance. He allowed the men to lay him along the block without protest.

The two men knelt down beside the altar, and the watchers stood round in a semicircle. Then, while the gong still tolled out its sombre rhythm, the businessmen unbuttoned their jackets and stripped off their suits. It was all accomplished so smoothly, so quickly. Underneath the pinstripes, the pure linen robes. They stood completely motionless before the altar, no longer businessmen but priests.

'What are they waiting for?'

'The Sun,' Rosanna said.

The gong stopped beating, and the men began to chant. The sun's rays glimmered gold along the tops of the columns, the trickle of light touching the dew with living warmth, turning the drops into flashing beads of light. Soon the rays would reach the altar and the victim.

The men knelt down and pressed their faces to the earth. An ancient priest, draped in a leopardskin ornamented with a golden leopard's head and golden claws, came from the Holy of Holies and approached the altar.

In his hands he held a long knife and a hatchet.

'This is it, boys,' Rosanna whispered. 'We have to do something *now*!'

Joey grasped her arm. 'Rosie, do you see who it is?'

She nearly cried out, and any last flickering hope that the police might arrive died in her. The high priest was Youssef.

He stood behind the altar as the dawn rays struck, facing the sun, his lips moving in prayer, the knife in his hand. Rosanna stood up and took a step forward. They still had not seen her.

Youssef raised the knife over Finbar's chest. The blade caught the sun, a solid ray of pure gold, as he held it high.

Rosanna cried out, a shrill, desperate cry. 'No! Stop! You mustn't do this!' She ran forward and flung herself across the altar stone, sheltering Finbar with her own body. She called his name; he didn't respond, but she felt his chest rise and subside in a deep sigh. He was alive, but Rosanna guessed he had been deeply hypnotised. He gave no sign that he was aware of her, or of what was happening.

'Look out, Rosie!' It was Joey's voice. Turning, Rosanna saw that Youssef's golden blade was turned on her.

'Leave him!' he hissed. 'The sacrifice must be made!'

As the blade began to descend, Joey hurled himself at Youssef and hung on to his arm like a terrier, while Rosanna struggled to pull Finbar off the altar block. Mike threw himself into the fray — but so did the priests, seizing Mike and roughly pinioning his arms. Rosanna screamed as Youssef freed himself and lunged, the glittering blade slicing towards Joey.

'Oh, no!'

Suddenly there was a shot — confusion, noise, bedlam — men running in every direction. Finbar still lying motionless on the block. Men in uniform filling the court. Joey twisting on the sand, doubled up with pain, a dark stain spreading from his arm. Youssef crumpling, with a burst of scarlet flowering from his chest. He toppled forward over Finbar's inert body.

The police were everywhere, chasing the fleeing priests.

Finbar was insensible, but otherwise unharmed. Saud wept as he pulled his uncle off the altar and lifted him into his arms. Youssef was not dead; but his eyes were glazing over.

'Why, Uncle? Why?' Saud sat holding him, cradling his head, rocking to and fro in shock and grief. Tears poured down his face. Youssef tried to pat his arm, but he was too weak.

'You have to ask?' he whispered.

'But why *you*?'

Youssef shrugged, and coughed blood. Rosanna stood by, helplessly watching. Youssef tried to raise his head.

'Ah. Miss Rose,' he said, with the trace of a smile. 'How clever. How did you know our secret? Who betrayed us?'

'No one,' she said. 'But you and your friends forgot one small thing. I found my doorway. I saw through to the other side.'

'You saw?' He coughed again. The red stain on his chest had become a flood.

'Youssef,' Rosanna said softly. 'Why was it necessary?'

'Blood for the land,' he muttered.

Rosanna gripped his arm and shook him desperately, striving to keep his soul with them. 'Youssef! Don't die! You were fooled! This has nothing to do with the land. You thought you were helping Rameses — but even Rameses is being used. He's been taken over by the Dark Power — by Set himself.'

Saud clutched his uncle close. Youssef's head fell back, but he was still alive.

'Where is Abu Samil?' Rosanna begged him. 'You must tell us, Youssef! Where is he?'

The dying man groaned. 'He promised me ...'

'Youssef!' she shrieked. His eyes went blank.

Saud wept, without shame, holding his uncle against him, cradling him like a baby. Rosanna wished the priest had been anyone but Youssef, and she wished it had been anyone but Saud who had killed him.

The rising sun began to fill the courtyard. Rosanna looked round at Joey — huddled on the sand of the Feast Hall, trembling with shock, blood pouring from the deep gash in his arm. But he was being looked after by the police, they had called an ambulance and would take him to a hospital. She turned back to Finbar, beginning to stir from his deep hypnotic trance upon the altar, his body — the body of a golden boy offered to the god — more beautiful than she had ever seen it. And once again, in a shining splinter of time, she knew the answer.

'Edfu!' she cried. 'The Hawk! We must go to the Temple of the Hawk. If he believes he's won at last, that's where he'll be!'

176

Chapter Twenty-Five

Hearing the car screech to a halt, four men stepped out of
the entrance to the Edfu temple complex and barred the way.
They were momentarily surprised to see Finbar clad only in
his pleated white linen skirt, but they had a duty to perform.

'I am sorry,' said their leader with a bow. 'It is not possible to visit now. The temple is not open for this day.'

'Get out of my way!' Finbar pushed him aside angrily.
The man hurried after him and grabbed his arms, none too
gently. Finbar spun round, freeing himself. The men were
alarmed and protested loudly. They went quiet when Saud
showed his policeman's armbands, but even then their
leader tried desperately to stop Finbar. He ran in front of
him and spread his arms wide.

'It is not possible, sirs!' he cried.

Finbar pierced him with a cold stare. 'You are in my way!'

The man was as nervous as a cat, but something made
him persist. Sweat stood out on his brow.

'I cannot let you pass!'

'Fool! You try to keep me from what is mine?'

Finbar put his hand to the ka-statue hanging round his
neck. The guard stepped back, his face grey with fear, his
eyes glued to the statue.

'Stand aside!'

The guard cringed as Finbar stood over him, eyes flashing.

'Look at me!' he said fiercely. 'Know me!'

The guard bowed. 'I know you, lord,' he said.

There was no further resistance. They hurried along the girdle wall to the gateway, the guards following.

Even before they reached the gateway, they could hear the sound of chanting. It was the paean of triumph.

But there was something else — a strange agonised shrieking that was not human. Rosanna shivered apprehensively. She had no idea what creature was making that horrendous sound, only that it was a living thing in torment. The four guards apparently decided that discretion was better than valour, and turned tail.

'Should I stop them?' Saud asked, waving his gun.

'They are nothing. Let them go. My business is here.'

Finbar turned, and they went into the courtyard.

A group of white-clad men, identical to those at Karnak, clustered round the granite statue of Horus. Leading the chanting, also swathed in priestly garb, was the opulent figure of Abu Samil. Round his balding head he wore a band of silver ribbon, tied at the back.

Embroidered across his chest was the outline of a strange animal unknown to man, a black creature with a long snout and wedge-shaped ears, which Rosanna could only identify from pictures in her books — since no human had ever seen such a beast. The image of Set, the Evil One, the Enemy.

In front of Abu Samil was a small table draped with a black velvet cloth, and on it were neatly laid a hatchet and a silver bowl. An acolyte stood nearby with a bowl of water and an incongruously modern white towel.

But the focus of attention was not Abu Samil the priest, nor the altar table, nor even a tall, hooded Nubian wearing a leather gauntlet. It was the outraged but still imperious desert hawk which flapped furiously upon his arm. Its legs were fettered, and a long silver chain bound it to the Nubian's wrist. It was obvious that this falcon was not about to be crowned in triumph. It had already been pierced to draw blood — which a white-clad youth caught in a small silver bowl — and its defiant cries tore the hot, still air. Its eyes spat hatred.

178

Saud moved forward with his gun, but Finbar stopped him. 'This fight is mine,' he said grimly. Saud nodded.

Finbar took another pace into the sun-baked courtyard. He lifted his head.

'Rameses!'

The word was both a recognition and a challenge. Abu Samil turned.

There was a deadly hush. The white-robed men fell back. The two faced each other across the square. Finbar walked forward, haughty, unafraid. The aura of the god was on him.

'You stand in my place,' he said coldly.

Abu Samil was taken aback, but regained his composure.

'My dear O'Neill,' he murmured. 'It seems you have caught me out in this little charade.'

'I'm sure you did not expect to see me.'

'We thought you were dead. How very delighted we are that it was all a mistake.'

'Your mistake,' replied Finbar.

Abu Samil stretched out a finger and ran it up and down the silver handle of the hatchet that lay on the altar table.

'I think not,' he said. He looked pointedly at the nearest of his acolytes. As if they had been given a signal, all the white-clad men drew knives. Rosanna gasped as she saw that all those robed figures wore square black rings.

They began, wolf-like, to circle in on Finbar. He snatched the Horus statue from his neck and held it high.

'Get back!' he shouted. 'You stand in the presence of the Avenger. Know where you are! Know who I am!'

Rosanna could not help staring at Abu Samil's face. It had twisted, creased into a mask of hatred and ugliness — Rameses possessed utterly by Set, the Devil.

'Don't hesitate, you fools!' he cried. 'Kill him now!'

'You do well to fear me,' said Finbar softly. 'Look around you. These men will not raise their hands against the Avenger.' He faced Abu Samil. 'It's just you and I, my friend, as it has always been, wherever I have found you.'

Abu Samil licked his lips. His acolytes muttered nervously and backed away, deserting their master. Finbar threw back his head and laughed in scorn.

'You wish to celebrate my death? Then why do you stand there, skulking behind an altar? Come out and fight me. Finish what you started, if you can.'

Abu Samil picked up the hatchet. A sinister smile played on his lips. He could see that Finbar stood before him unarmed.

'Come, then, and I will give your flesh to the vultures!'

'Finbar! Use this!' Rosanna's voice came between them for a second. There was a ring and clatter of metal as she threw the iron spike Mike had picked up at Karnak, but it landed uselessly, too far to Finbar's right.

Before he had the chance to pick it up Abu Samil charged at him, the hatchet scything the air. Finbar dropped nimbly to one knee, measuring the distance. As Abu Samil drew back his arm to strike, Finbar threw himself at him with all his weight. Their two bodies met, and Abu Samil was caught off balance. He began to topple, with Finbar gripping his arm, and they went down together. Abu Samil cursed: the razor-sharp blade had slashed his thigh as they fell. First blood to Finbar.

Finbar got to one knee and hauled the panting Abu Samil to his feet. The pause was only a moment. With a grunt like an animal's, Abu Samil came for him, head down, arms flailing. The silver ribbon was dragged off as his head hit Finbar full force in the solar plexus. Finbar's breath whistled with the pain, but it did not drop him. As Abu Samil's head came up Finbar hit him hard, a left, then a right to the chin. He was rocked backwards. Finbar came in then, not giving him a chance. Abu Samil buckled, and went down.

But he was not finished. As Finbar bent to heave him up once more, Abu Samil flung a handful of dust full in his face, and at the same time lashed out with his legs to tangle Finbar's and bring him down. Finbar twisted sideways, trying to protect his kidneys, as his enemy leapt up and started to kick. Red mists of pain clouded his vision.

Abu Samil stepped back and laughed. He had the iron spike in his hand, the jagged point aimed at Finbar's throat.

Finbar lay very still, watching his enemy. A bitter smile touched his lips. This was the House of the Piercing, where Horus had defeated and slain the Evil One; but this time it was Abu Samil who held the spear.

Rosanna knew she would have to move fast. She picked up a rock and began to edge forward. The hawk saw her, and began to rattle its silver chain. She willed it to keep still.

For the second time Finbar was staring death in the face, but this time he was fully conscious. Hatred burned in his eyes. Even though he had known that Youssef had intended to kill him, he had also realised that Youssef, for all his faults, represented the ancient cult for good and not for evil. He had stood for the old powers of fertility.

Abu Samil was not interested in the living land. He was the incarnation of evil, the power of the Dark Brother. They had been enemies through all time.

Youssef had been considerate, even apologetic, to his prisoner. He had studied Finbar, seen that he was a man to be admired, and assured him that had he not been chosen for the role he must play, he would have been proud to have called him his friend. He would see to it that Finbar died with dignity and nobility, he said. There would be no suffering, nothing to spoil the final sacrifice.

'I quite understand that you do not wish to die,' Youssef had said gently. 'That is because your western character has influenced you. You have forgotten. But this is not your fault — we do not blame you.'

'The soil doesn't need my blood!' Finbar had said.

'On the contrary, it is a thirsty, thirsty soil. If it were not so, why did Osiris die? The seed must fall into the ground before it can sprout and rise. Hold the little husk in your hand, away from the soil, and it is a useless, dry thing. Let it die as a seed, and who can guess what wondrous thing it might come to be?'

'Why not settle for the blood of an ox?'

'Sometimes. If we cannot find what we are looking for. But you will understand when it is done. You have the Horus-ka. You have been touched by it, and you cannot go back to what you were before.'

Youssef had made it seem an honour, to be chosen to die.

But now it was Abu Samil who stood over him, sneering, panting, jabbing the spike mockingly at his throat, toying with him like a cat tormenting a vole. His eyes shone and an atmosphere of pure malice oozed from him, desecrating the courtyard. As Rosanna drew closer and closer, a strange, malevolent stillness hung over the place. There was a tension in the stones, in the air, in the dark shrines.

Rosanna struck the Nubian a blow on the back of the skull, with all her strength, and he went down. The hawk flapped into the air, straining at its leash, the courtyard ringing with its unearthly shrieks.

The chain gave at a weak link, and the enraged creature was free. It soared upwards and hung in the still air, giving vent to its fierce hunting cries. It was poised directly over Abu Samil's head.

'Strike! Strike!' Rosanna cried. Abu Samil looked up, and was blinded by the sun. He flailed the spike desperately. The hawk dropped, straight as an arrow, to his face. Abu Samil screamed as the beak and talons ripped at him, gouging into soft flesh. He dropped the spike and beat at the bird with his hands.

It was easy, now, for Finbar to dive sideways and pick up the spike. In a second his fingers curled round the cold metal and sent a spattering of rusty flakes flickering to the dust.

The House of the Piercing rang with Abu Samil's cries of agony as he tore the hawk away from his face and flung it down, breaking its wing.

Finbar circled towards him, holding the spike in both hands. Abu Samil, coughing and gagging, was trampling the wounded hawk as it flapped its one good wing helplessly, the other trailing in the bloodstained dust.

'Set!' Finbar whispered hoarsely.

Abu Samil spun back to face him, the blood from his wounds turning his face into a mask of horror.

'Well?' he sneered. 'You have the weapon now. Why do you not use it? What are you waiting for? You weak fool — you haven't the power to defeat me. You will never win the battle, you thorn in my flesh, you usurper!'

'I never took what was not mine.'

'Never?' Blood trickled from the glistening dome of his head. 'You have always begrudged me my power, my strength. You *little* man — what did you think you could ever achieve against me?'

'Justice,' said Finbar quietly. He lifted the spike.

The watchers were very still, breath caught in their throats, as Finbar took another step towards his ancient enemy. The acolytes were silent watchers now, none lifting a hand to intervene.

Rosanna's body felt as if it were stretched taut as wire. She ran to Finbar's side.

'Keep back!' he shouted, keeping his eyes on Abu Samil.

'This time we stand together!' she cried.

Abu Samil charged at Finbar like a goaded bull. His hands seized the spike, and they began to grapple to and fro across the courtyard.

Rosanna summoned up all her power, all her strength. The drumming was back in her ears, the hiss and rush of blood.

A sickening noise, and a crack ripped its way across the open space, zigzagging amongst the stones. Stones that had taken eight men to set in place were pulled apart as if they were no more than wet paper.

Rosanna put out a hand into the air in front of her, groping for something, anything, with which to steady herself. There was nothing. She swayed and fell, the rough stone grazing her knees and palms.

Stone which should have been firm was trembling,

humming with tension. Beneath the stone — filling her and emanating from her — surged a tremendous power.

An ominous rumbling sound came from the dark ruins. Something — a huge block — cracked with a sound like a rifle shot. Some of the white-robed priests were on their knees, gabbling incoherently, their eyes wild, looking about desperately for some avenue of escape; but they did not know which way to turn to find safety.

The courtyard heaved. It was as if the massive stones were no more than a thin skin over some mighty monster straining to be let loose.

Finbar twisted the spike and sent Abu Samil to the ground. His head met the stone with a sickening thud. Raising the bar like a spear, Finbar poised himself for the kill. Behind him, deep in the shrine, the statue of Horus strode with his spear over his pierced enemy.

Afterwards, when Rosanna was trying to piece together in her mind the incredible events, it seemed impossible that it had all taken just a few seconds. A thousand ages came crashing in, rolling together into that eternal moment.

One instant, the temple was in the grip of the tremor; the next, it was still.

There was an eerie, nerve-racking silence. No sound. No movement. Then the dark shadow of the Hawk of Edfu began to move, looming over the helpless Abu Samil as he lay gasping at its feet. He looked up, transfixed like a rabbit in the glare of a headlight.

With the ominous grating of stone on stone, the huge ka-statue of the Avenger was moving, shifting, toppling forward.

Finbar leaped back, the iron bar clattering to the ground. There was one great crash as the Hawk fell, cutting off Abu Samil's last choking scream. His outstretched hand clenched once, and then was still. A final little wrench of the earth, a last trickle of falling stones and mortar, and the battle was over. The sun shone through the dust, which was already sinking to the ground from whence it came.

Chapter Twenty-Six

Back in Cairo, they were all tired, and tempers were frayed. Rosanna was depressed. What had happened so far away in Upper Egypt no longer seemed real. But it had been real. Appallingly real.

Joey was gone; his parents, after one chaotic telephone call, had insisted he should take the first flight home. Rosanna had seen him off, early in the morning; she had hugged him goodbye, careful not to jar his wounded arm, and they had promised to write. She knew already that they would not keep that promise. This trip, for both of them, had been time-out-of-time, far from their ordinary lives; for Joey that time-out-of-time had ended, and for Rosanna it was already beginning to end.

The Professor had not been allowed to leave Aswan, and his future was very much in doubt. It was hoped that the Government could be persuaded to be lenient, in view of his previous services to Egypt, but there were no guarantees.

Well, Rosanna thought, he had got no more than he deserved. And yet — who was she to moralise? Everyone had their failings, their weaknesses. No, she could afford to feel some pity for the poor old Professor, and was glad that at least he would be spared the nightmare of the photographic evidence of his folly being made public. Saud had given them his word on that. He would see to it that the incriminating evidence disappeared permanently.

'It is no problem,' he had said. 'Leave it to me.'

He had seen the group safely onto the overnight train to Cairo, while Finbar had spent an entire day helping the police with their inquiries. Poor Finbar, Rosanna thought.

He flew in during the early afternoon, while the gang were either sunbathing peacefully on the hotel roof or trooping round the bazaar for final purchases. He went straight to his bed and slept for hours. Rosanna did not want to disturb him, but she left a message at the desk, saying that she was up on the roof, if he wanted to know. And that was where she stayed, watching flights of old-fashioned little red and white kites sailing over the acres of dun tenement blocks. On the adjacent roof a boy unlocked his pigeons from ramshackle cages and sent them wheeling over the city. He sat on the edge of the roof, holding a stick with a bunch of white rags tied to it, and watched them soar and dip. After a while he waved the stick, and the white rags guided them home.

Finbar came up just before dinner, looking for her. They sat in silence, looking at the ground, for a long time.

At length Finbar gave a deep sigh, and took Rosanna's hand. His eyes were evasive. Her heart gave a lurch. She could not see there what she had prayed so desperately to see.

And what did he see when he looked at her? A tired, battered London girl, switching off from her holiday and working out her timetable for her return to normality. She had to decide what to do, and quickly. The rest of the group, after they had had a few days to rest and recuperate, were heading off to Alexandria, to end the adventure with a few days by the sea. And Finbar was going to pull out. His job was done.

'Our last night,' he said, very softly. The ache in Rosanna's heart was so intense she felt physically sick. He was clenching her hand so tightly that it hurt.

'Yes.' Only a few more hours, and her time-out-of-time would be over. She wanted to see into his eyes — across an eternity of shifting sands, into the inscrutable depths of a prince's eyes. They both knew that it was hopeless. This was all they had.

He put his hands on her arms, and her mouth met his fiercely. She clung to him, locked herself against him, desperate with hunger for him.

'Hey!' he said mockingly. 'I didn't know you'd be so pleased to see me. Go gently with me, I've had quite a pounding. I'm a fragile boy.'

'I'm sorry,' she mumbled. Sorry it has to end like this. Sorry, so sorry, that you don't want me after all. Sorry we ever met — no, not that. Never that. What would her life have been if she had never met him?

He squeezed her shoulders — a paternal squeeze, an uncle cuddling his favourite niece.

'You deserve a treat,' he said. 'I've a little plan for us. Something I know you want to do.'

'Oh?' Her scintillating attempts at conversation. 'What plan?'

'Do you think you could bear to see another dawn?'

One last dawn. Sacrifice at dawn.

'Why?'

'I'm not going to tell you. It's a secret. Trust me, Rosie?' His blue eyes smouldered.

'Sure.'

Nothing sure in this universe.

'I'll be waiting on your landing at three o'clock a.m. Slip out and meet me then.'

Hope flashed in her eyes. Foolish, desperate hope. She swallowed hard, certain that he would see and laugh at her.

'What's the matter? Don't you want to come with me?'

'Oh, yes, Finbar.'

Anywhere. To the ends of the earth.

* * *

The velvet dark and the huge stars had vanished in the morning mist. Finbar sent the taxi away, and led Rosanna through the necropolis to the Great Pyramid. Everything was wet with dew. They passed the stables at the foot of the plateau, where the horses and camels still dozed, waiting for the new day.

'Where's the guard?'

'I've bought them off. It's *our* pyramid.'

They had the world to themselves. They walked through the mist, their shoes scrunching on grit, padding on sand. They reached the limestone mountain. A breeze shifted the swirls of mist. Rosanna shivered. For the first time in Egypt, she was actually cold.

Below and above them everything was hidden. Only the huge blocks confronting them were visible. The rest was swathed in grey.

Finbar led the way, and hauled Rosanna up behind him. She got the impression he knew what he was doing.

'You've done this before, I take it,' she panted, when they paused for a rest. Finbar laughed. He knew she wanted to know what he was thinking, but he would give nothing away. Probably right. A mistake to make this real. Keep it time-out-of-time.

Soon the climb became dirty. Fingers sank into an accumulation of debris, surprising evidence of the creatures to whom this great pile was home. Neat brown and white falcon-feathers, black tattered quills of crows. White droppings everywhere, spatters of owl or vulture, small bones, rats' skins. Then, in the silence, the cackle of a bird resenting their disturbance, launching itself into the mist and vanishing.

Then, abruptly, the mist shining, becoming golden. They were like deep-sea divers coming to the surface, heads breaking through and bobbing in the sun. Above them nothing but the narrowing mountainside, and the blue sky. They climbed out of the mist and felt the sun, hot already, on their backs.

Rosanna was giddy if she looked up, so she kept her eyes on the block ahead. Block after mountainous block, step after long step; knees grazed, hands sore, legs aching, sweat pulled away by the intermittent breeze.

Until there were no more blocks, and they lay, triumphant, on the roof of the world. They rested, flat on their backs, under nothing but the sky, caressed by sun and silence, detached from the world. Below them, Chephren's peak, and Mycerinus, and the little pyramids; and beyond them, the vastness of the desert.

'Where's Mark Twain's book?' Rosanna asked.

'Wrong pyramid.'

She slipped into Finbar's arms with a sigh, and he held her against him. Close. So close. She was aware of every inch of him.

She memorised the feel of him. It was all she would have, and it would have to last her a lifetime.

Voices floated up from the desert, a long way off. They sat with their legs dangling over the edge, and watched the landscape start to move. In the east, a train of camels leaving the broad table-land, each bearing a heavy burden but moving so fast that the little donkeys were hard put to keep up with them. In the fertile valley, the fellahin and their oxen drifting to the fields. Cars edging down the road from the town. Over everything, the sun.

Finbar looked at Rosanna. There was a strange tightness in his expression that she could not interpret. He held her hand, but his spirit had withdrawn again. She could sense it, just from his eyes and the touch of his hand. He was going, and she could not keep him.

Time had run out.

Rosanna fought desperately to maintain the last shreds of her dignity. It was vital, somehow, that he should not see her cry. Now that he was out of danger, he didn't want her. Perhaps he never had.

'I suppose this is it, then, Rosie.'

'Yes. I suppose it is.'

After all those centuries. Joy after so much pain, and then pain again. How could this be it? How could he sit on his island, and just let her drift away in the stream? How could the gods have allowed her just that one tiny glimpse of happiness, twisted their lifelines together, and then pulled them apart again?

'Goodbye, my dear.'

He had said it.

'Goodbye.'

She clamped her grief down tight.

* * *

Rosanna sat next to a Pakistani salesman and his son. The child was tearful and looked as if he had a temperature. She tried conversation, but the child did not speak English and the man did not appear to welcome it. The air hostess was solicitous, plied them with food and drinks and offered duty-free packets of cigarettes.

'Going home, dear?' she asked. Rosanna nodded. Yes, she was going home. She had almost forgotten that she had a home, and a family, and a humdrum boring life that ticked through the slow drag of hours from sleep to sleep.

'Had a nice trip, then?' The woman's blonde curls bobbed forward over her carefully-made-up face. The Pakistani salesman watched them bounce up and down with a fascinated stare. Her red lips smiled, widely. 'Holiday, was it? Up the Nile?'

Rosanna nodded. Across the aisle ladies of indeterminate age, wrapped in black shawls, peeped at the blonde.

'Ooh, a holiday. Very nice.'

Rosanna subsided into her seat, grateful when the hostess moved along, her hips swaying up the aisle.

A tourist-class flight via Belgrade and Zagreb, the cheapest and earliest flight available. Just like Cinderella:

get away from the ball before the footmen turn to mice and the glittering coach resolves itself into a pumpkin again. Cut and run. Take care to leave no glass slippers behind.

Glass slippers. That made her smile, bitterly. Before she left Cairo she had taken her sandals, grey with powdered sand, and slipped them into a polythene bag. Battered sandals that had taken her all through Egypt, touched the soil, stood in the tombs of pharaohs. If she treasured them, never wore them again, cherished the fragile grains that clung to them — mightn't they act as ka-sandals and bring her back?

Tears glittered in her eyes. It was stupid of her to cling to any of it, even a few grains of sand. She would soon be back in her proper place, her proper time. No more gods, no more signs, no more Finbar. And the knowledge of it, the hopelessness of it, brought with it such piercing pain.

She gripped her arm tight across her empty heart. What was the use? There was no point in torturing herself like this. Things had happened, and now they were to unhappen. She had to go back home. She was already halfway to being back.

It was nearly twelve hours after leaving Cairo that Rosanna left the plane, exhausted, at Heathrow. She hurried through the checkouts. Through the windows she could see the rain, the slow, soft drizzle of familiar grey London. The same old London she had left just a couple of weeks ago. Nothing had changed. She was vaguely conscious of a longing for bacon, baked beans, fried eggs, milk. And sleep. She could sleep for a month. She headed off towards the Customs.

There was a tall dark man lounging against the far wall. In the instant before she realised he was a stranger, Rosanna's heart lurched. She had to learn to control these wild imaginings. She slapped her feelings down, fearing that if she tried to walk through the green channel with guilt stamped all over her face she would be hauled back by

191

the officials. Yes, there was one looking her over right now, with an accusing stare. Was she trying to smuggle hashish? Was she gun-running for some terrorist group? Any minute now he would pounce and subject her to a third-degree interrogation. Yet she had nothing to declare; except, of course, that her whole life had changed, and she did not know what lay ahead of her.

The official was looking past her. He had not even really noticed her. It was all her imagination. Rosanna sighed, and shuffled down the line.

She reached the meeting point where her mother should have been waiting, but it didn't take her long to realise that no one was there. She went miserably to the desk to see if there was any message for her.

There were two. Her mother's note said that she'd been held up and Rosie should go get a coffee and wait.

The second note had been faxed through from Egypt. It was from Finbar.

'I couldn't let you go away thinking I didn't care about you. You know me — too many problems, too many traumas. But I swear to you, we'll be together again someday. Just give me a little time. We found each other across thousands of miles and thousands of years — we'll surely find each other again.'

Rosanna read the note until she knew it by heart. Then she folded it carefully and slipped it into the plastic bag which held her sandals. She hoisted her bag firmly onto her shoulders, took a deep breath, and headed for the Waiting Area.